LAST WALK AT RUSSELL COVE

Know your friends well before you join them in the lottery.

Howard Blair

HOWARD G. BLAIR

Outskirts Press, Inc.
Denver, Colorado

This is a work of fiction. The events and characters described herein are imaginary and are not intended to refer to specific places or living persons. The opinions expressed in this manuscript are solely the opinions of the author and do not represent the opinions or thoughts of the publisher. The author has represented and warranted full ownership and/or legal right to publish all the materials in this book.

Last Walk at Russell Cove
All Rights Reserved.
Copyright © 2008 Howard G. Blair
V3.0

This book may not be reproduced, transmitted, or stored in whole or in part by any means, including graphic, electronic, or mechanical without the express written consent of the publisher except in the case of brief quotations embodied in critical articles and reviews.

Outskirts Press, Inc.
http://www.outskirtspress.com

ISBN: 978-1-4327-2930-1

Outskirts Press and the "OP" logo are trademarks belonging to Outskirts Press, Inc.

PRINTED IN THE UNITED STATES OF AMERICA

ACKNOWLEDGMENTS

Several individuals have assisted me with this story. My college fraternity brother John Bejarano got me going with the idea, and had some good suggestions. His wife Katy not only encouraged me, gave me some constructive criticism, but was kind enough to do the editing. This job took her hours, for which I am very grateful. A couple of other people who contributed ideas for the story were another college fraternity brother, Bob Testa, and my neighbor Bill Evans.

I also need to thank my wife, Pat. She put up with endless hours of me talking about the story, changing the story and completing the novel. She also read a draft of the book and pointed out several areas that needed clarification or changing.

CAST OF MAIN CHARACTERS

Fred and Ginger Bellows: Fred is a retired land developer living in the Sacramento, CA area.

George and Debbie Mitchell: George is a retired farm equipment salesman living in the Fresno, CA area.

Dr. Jim and Linda Schroeder: Jim is a semi-retired heart surgeon, living in the Sacramento, CA area.

Tom and Pam Decker: Living in Reno, NV. Tom is still working as an advertising executive.

Dave and Norma Wheeler: Dave is a retired financial officer living in Glendale, CA, West of Pasadena.

PROLOGUE

It was 8:30 am when Dave Wheeler stepped out of the rental house and headed for his car. Dave was sixty-seven years old and just over six feet. He had held his weight to around 185 pounds by eating right, running and doing some weight lifting. His hair was thinning but he still had a full head of iron gray, wavy locks. As usual in the coastal area of Northern California, his car was covered with heavy dew from the night before. As Dave entered his car, he heard George Mitchell come out of the house and head for the passenger door. Dave started the engine as George entered beside him.

"OK, let's go down and pick up our winnings," George said. George was a large boned man with a ruddy complexion; a long time friend of Dave's and was also just turning sixty-seven. He carried his 230 pounds fairly well on his six foot two frame, but he was getting soft around the middle and it showed through his light jacket.

"We've been doing this for fifteen years and have not won anything yet," Dave responded, as the engine was warming up. He turned on the wipers to get the dew off the front windows.

"I know, but I have a feeling this time will be different," George replied.

Dave Wheeler didn't say anything as he turned on the rear window heater. He then lowered and raised both the driver's side window and the passenger window hoping the window seals would scrape enough dew off so he could see out of both sides. As he started to back out of the driveway George kept talking. "You never know what this weather is going to be up here at Russell Cove. Hell, it could be beautiful in September or colder than shit. Right now it's on the shit side. What kind of car is this anyway?"

"It's a BMW 740Li," Dave responded, as he backed out of the

driveway trying to see if the road was clear. As he straightened out the car and started down the hill toward the road to town, George once again could not keep his thoughts from spilling out of his mouth.

"Nice car. Lots of gadgets to play with. I see there isn't anyone on the golf course this time of day. By-the-way, Norma still looks good for her age." Norma was Dave Wheeler's wife of 45 years.

"So does your Debbie," Dave responded. His thoughts did a quick flash back to his college days when he used to date Debbie. They had made love twice, once while he was going with her and once just before she became engaged to George, as he had talked her into one more romp in the sack before she got married. Dave knew that Debbie never told George of their coupling.

Dave remembered that day in college like it was yesterday. He was studying in the library one evening when Debbie came in wearing a white Angora sweater and a black tight skirt. They had gone together for six months but broke it off about a year ago when they decided their personalities were not going to be right for the long run. Both were physically attracted to each other and had made love once before they called it quits. Since then Debbie had gone with George Bellows, and there was talk of them getting engaged.

Debbie noticed Dave in the library, smiled and sat down about two tables away from him. She opened her books and started reading. Dave could not take his eyes off her and watched her cross her legs under the table. The short skirt revealed lots of thigh and Dave felt the blood rush through his body. He sat there thinking about her for the next two hours, looking at the way the sweater fit across her breasts and the smoothness of her shapely legs. When she closed her book and got up to leave, Dave did the same and caught up with her as she was going out the library door.

"Going back to the dorm?" he asked.

"Yes, I've done enough studying for tonight," she responded.

"My car is in the parking lot behind the Chemistry building. I can give you a ride," he said, trying to keep his eyes off her sweater.

"It's a nice night, and I can walk, but thanks anyway Dave."

"Come on Debbie, I'm not going to bite, not much anyway," he said trying to be clever. "I'll take you straight to the dorm."

She looked at him for a moment and relented and said, "All right."

They walked the short distance to the Chemistry building parking lot and got in the car.

"You really look good tonight," Dave said. "You know how I love Angora sweaters. They are so soft and smooth."

"Just take me back to the dorm, please."

"Look, one little kiss for old times sake will not hurt anything. Please, you look so nice and I do miss you."

"You know I'm going with George, and we're getting serious. I don't think it would be a good idea for us to get involved again."

He leaned close to her and felt her hair tickle his face. "One more time will not hurt. Damn you smell good. Don't you trust me?"

"I don't trust myself," she said not moving away.

Dave slowly moved his mouth until it was over hers. They touched tongues, and he felt her responding to him. He put his hand on her calf and started rubbing her leg up to the inside of her thigh. He felt himself get stiff and hard.

"Damn you," she said but did nothing to stop him.

"We need to move to the back seat," he said and without waiting reached across and opened her door. She started to get out, and Dave sprung back to the driver's door, quickly opened it and got in the back seat. They once again embraced, and he slid his right hand up under her sweater in the back and unsnapped her bra. He lifted the sweater up over her breasts and started kissing them. At the same time he moved his hand between her legs and felt her wetness. He backed off and unzipped his trousers and let his stiff penis emerge from his pants. He took his fingers and once again stroked her until she was moaning. He stretched her panties away from the front of her vagina and entered her, not moving for a moment but just enjoying the sensation. Debbie started moving her hips rhythmically in short upper movements which drove Dave wild. They started moving together and before long both were moaning, kissing and caressing. As Dave started to ejaculate, Debbie pushed him hard backwards, forcing his penis out of her. He quickly put his penis back in his pants, pressed up against her and felt the wetness cover his underwear.

"I'm not getting pregnant at this point in my life!" Debbie exclaimed.

"Damn, Debbie, that was not fair," Dave said as he tried to calm himself.

Dave remembered the empty feeling he had when she started putting her bra back on. He thought if he could have it do to over again, things would have been different. Dave thought to himself that he wished he'd gotten Debbie a few more times since then. Maybe there will be a possibility while they are all in Russell Cove.

"Dave, don't forget the stop sign!" George said in one of his loud voices.

Dave came out of his thoughts about Debbie and noticed he was going a little fast toward the stop sign. He pushed hard on the brakes and the car came to a stop. Dave sat there for a minute trying to get Debbie out of his mind.

"You OK, Dave?" George asked.

"Yeah, I'm OK. Just lost in thought for a few moments." He turned on to highway US-1 that led to the small town of Russell Cove.

In the mid 1800's, Russell Cove was a small port for providing fish to the growing city of San Francisco. Now it was a primarily a fishing village of around fifty people, with its main industry being the tourists that visited almost year around. The town was just North of Bodega Bay, made famous by Alfred Hitchcock's movie, *The Birds*, filmed back in 1963. In the mid 1980's a developer saw the potential of building some homes in a hilly area near the cove. The development was similar to the one built just outside of Bodega Bay. The houses were quickly sold out as the area was quiet, away from the rush of every day life, and very relaxing. The only drawback, if there was any, was the weather was generally overcast, and the area had lots of rain, as it was on the Pacific North Coast. A lot of the home owners had purchased the houses as second homes, using them in the summer months to get away from the heat of the interior. As expected, many of the houses were available to rent for visitors coming to that area during the winter and fall months.

Each year Dave, George, their wives and three other couples rented a five bedroom house for four days in the fall. The five couples came to Russell Cove just to get away, drink, eat, play golf relax and enjoy each other's company. All five couples were college friends, and had known each other for almost forty years. There were two traditions they followed each year. The first was a morning walk. Each morning they all would take a walk around the housing complex, which took about an hour and a half. The second was for each couple to contribute a dollar to a kitty used to purchase a California lottery ticket. Once purchased, they would sit around for a few hours talking about what they would do with the money once they had won. This morning Dave and George were going to the village to purchase a newspaper and check the numbers on the lottery ticket that had been purchased the night before.

"Do you know where Jim bought the ticket yesterday?" George asked Dave as they were coming into the village.

"He told me to look for a gas station on the left side of the road as you enter town. There should be a lottery sign hanging in the window. You can get a paper there also," Dave said.

"There it is," pointed out George as he discovered the filling station.

Dave guided the car into a parking spot away from the filling tanks and stopped the car.

"No need for both of us to go in," Dave said. "I'll wait here and you get the paper and come on back, and we'll check the numbers. I have the ticket here in my pocket." George got out of the car and went into the store.

George came out of the store with two newspapers. As he entered the car Dave pulled out the ticket. George fumbled with the paper until he found the lottery section and said, "Which lottery are we playing?"

Dave told him the California SuperLotto.

"OK, here are the numbers: 21, 10, 33, 12, 5 and the mega number is 38."

"Read them again," Dave said as he felt his heart start to race.

"21, 10, 33, 12, 5 and 38," George repeated.

"Let me see the paper," Dave said as he almost jerked the paper out of George's hand.

"Son of a bitch," Dave mumbled. "I think we won the bastard."

"What!" George exclaimed. "Let me see the ticket. It says here the amount is twenty-one million dollars."

Both men sat in the car in silence for a moment looking at the numbers. Letting a large breath of air out of his lungs, George said, "Let me have the ticket, and I'll run it through the lottery machine in the store. That way it will verify we won so there will not be any question."

"No, we don't want to do that yet," Dave said. "Let's see what the others want to do. If you run the ticket through the machine then everyone will know that we won, and who knows what kind of press we'll get. We have time to think this over and plan a little before we announce it to the world."

"At least let's find a liquor store and get a few bottles of champagne so we can have a big celebration when we get back to the house," said George.

"We can do that as I think there is a small grocery store just around the corner," responded Dave.

"Son of a Bitch, isn't this something?" George said almost to himself. "Twenty-one million big ones. Let's see, split five ways is a little over 4 million. Take it in quick cash and take out the taxes and it will probably still be close to over a million each. Man oh man, won't the rest of the gang be surprised."

One million each will not be enough, Dave thought as he pulled back on the road and headed toward the grocery store. His thoughts went to Jack Williams and the next briefcase full of money. *I'll need a lot more than a million dollars. I need to think how I can get the split down to one or two couples, even if it means I have to kill some of my friends.*

CHAPTER 1

ONE DAY EARLIER

Dave Wheeler enjoyed driving roads like the one he was traveling. It was a two-lane road that was squeezed by rolling hills and blind corners. Dave guided his two-year-old BMW 740Li smoothly around the road at ten miles above the speed limit. He had just purchased the car about a year ago, and this was the first trip in this car to Russell Cove. It only had twelve thousand miles on it when he took possession. He was thinking about his retirement situation when he came up behind a slow moving truck and had to command the car to slow down as it moved closer to the truck.

"There is no rush," his wife Norma commented as she looked up over her glasses that she wore while reading. "We can't get into the house until after three o'clock anyway, and it's only one thirty."

"I know," Dave replied, "but its difficult keeping this monster down."

He glanced over and noticed that Norma went back to reading her book. She was still an attractive woman, Dave thought. They had been married for forty-five years, and he still enjoyed looking at her and watching her in her daily activities. She had put on a little weight around the hips, but her figure was still good for a woman of her age, and she dressed and carried herself well. Generally the first hour of a driving trip she and Dave had some general conversation, but after a while she donned her reading glasses and dissolved back into her book. Dave looked back at the road and began getting lost in his own thoughts.

Dave and Norma Wheeler were married three weeks after graduating from college. He had gone through the ROTC program at school and went in the Army for two years. They had been stationed in Germany and enjoyed the experience very much. After the Army he and Norma had moved to Los Angeles, and he took a job as an accountant for a large company. They had two daughters. Both of the girls had finished college several years ago and had good jobs. Both were married, but so far did not have any children. After he retired they had purchased a house in Glendale, an area just west of Pasadena, California. The house was smaller than the one they had lived in while raising their family and was in a semi-retirement community. Norma was involved in a lot of volunteer activities, and Dave occupied his time assisting people with their taxes and playing golf.

Each year when they went to Russell Cove to be with their friends, they preferred to drive up rather than fly. From Glendale the drive could be done in one day, but Dave and Norma Wheeler usually took two days to make the trip. They enjoyed the drive up Interstate 5 through the fertile valley of central California. The farms through this valley probably fed half the world. Dave had his favorite spots to watch for as he was driving along. He enjoyed driving over the Grapevine, the last mountain between southern California and the central valley area. Although the climb only reached about 4000 feet, it was steep enough that many times during the winter it was closed down due to a quarter or half inch of snow. Dave and Norma both got a chuckle each time they passed the exit for Lost Hills, Pumpkin Center and Buttonwillow.

About three hours from Glendale was the Harris Ranch. Both Dave and Norma liked to stay in the hotel that was part of the ranch and eat in the dining room. The next morning they knew they could reach Russell Cove in about four hours.

Although it was a bit further, the couple enjoyed taking the route that put them in the middle of San Francisco on their way to crossing the Golden Gate Bridge. They would turn off from Interstate 5 and go across to Highway 101 via the San Luis Rey reservoir coming out at Gilroy, the garlic capital of the world. Highway 101 took them up the coast past San Jose, Palo Alto and a host of other cities before they reached San Francisco. Norma Wheeler grew up in Redwood City, which was one of the cities along the highway. She enjoyed the warm feeling as she passed her

LAST WALK AT RUSSELL COVE

former living area.

Highway 101 goes through San Francisco on city streets to get to the Golden Gate Bridge. This area of the trip was one of the few times Norma put down her book and looked at the sights going past the window. She loved Van Ness Avenue in The City, and looked forward to passing Pacific Heights and going across the bridge. The view from the bridge was spectacular, if the weather was right. She could see the former prison Alcatraz and the skyline of San Francisco. Looking north, she could see the northern hills and a little of Sausalito.

About an hour north of San Francisco, the route took Dave and Norma off the four-lane highway and put them on a two-lane road, which was what they were driving at this hour, about twenty minutes out of Russell Cove.

Dave had started his career working for a large company as an accounting clerk. After about ten years with the large company, Dave's career reached a dead end. He started looking for a different opportunity with a small, family owned business. He got a job with Stills Distributors in northern Los Angeles and stayed with them for seventeen years, the last five as their Chief Financial Officer. Stills Distributors was a family owned company, currently operated by the son of the founder, who was generally doing lots of extracurricular activities rather than running the business. He put total trust in Dave, which proved to be an opportunity for Dave to build his retirement asset base. Dave's salary wasn't all that bad at one hundred and twenty thousand a year, but it was not enough to enjoy the life style that he and Norma wanted to have after retirement. Dave figured out a way to make more money by taking advantage of the inattention of the owner.

Dave's thoughts came back to the truck he was following when a small roadster car came up behind him. He and Norma were on their way to Russell Cove, which was about 75 miles north of San Francisco.

Dave took advantage of a break in traffic and passed the truck just north of the little town of Two Rock, an old Coast Guard station about ten miles from Bodega Bay on Bodega Ave.

Dave remembered the history of this area and thought about Two Rock, which was first called Dos Piedras, meaning two rocks in English. It was a landmark along the ancient Indian trail that ran from Bodega Bay to the inland valleys along the ridgelines and high ground. The trail was used by early Spanish explores traveling to and from Bodega Bay and San Francisco. In 1853 a United States post office was established there, and today it is not much more than a fork in the road. A lot of history is prevalent in the Two Rock Valley and much traveling was done along the trail, which became a rough map for Highway 1, along the coast of northern California. He thought one of the people who was going to Russell Cove grew up in the area, but he couldn't remember which one.

Dave Wheeler noticed the roadster also passed the truck and stayed close behind. He put pressure on the accelerator to increase his speed somewhat, hoping to increase the distance between his car and the roadster, and at the same time not get the attention and criticism from Norma. No such luck on both accounts. The roadster remained close, and Norma once again reminded him they were in no rush. Dave gave up, relaxed and let the roadster overtake him. As it did the driver sounded his car horn, and Dave recognized the individual in the car. It was George Mitchell, the husband of one of the couples they were meeting in Russell Cove. He did not remember that George had purchased a small sports type car, which looked like a Nissan "Z" model. The sound of the horn startled Norma, and she frowned at the car as it went by.

"There goes George," she remarked. "George was always the kind looking for attention and some things never change. I wonder where Debbie is?" Debbie was George's wife who was also expected at the cove, but was not in the car with George.

Dave once again put his attention to the road and began to get lost in his thoughts. He had been comfortable with his station in life and his economical situation until six months ago when he received a phone call from Jack Williams. That phone call completely destroyed Dave's composure and threatened his future.

His thoughts took him back five years ago when he was worried about his retirement. He calculated that his investments would only be three hundred and fifty thousand dollars when he retired. He would receive no money from the company, as it did not have a retirement plan. If he added social security to the anticipated interest to his investment, he figured he would run out of money in about ten years. He had to do something to supplement his income. He thought he found a perfect solution.

Stills Distributors did a total annual volume of around five hundred million per year. They had six stores in the Los Angeles area. Their facilities manager, who was a friend of the family, generally came to work half drunk. Dave noticed early on that the repair and maintenance expenses were generally very high but no one seemed to pay attention to them. His policy was to personally see and approve all payable checks above five thousand dollars. During a particular high volume month two years ago, Dave submitted an invoice for five thousand two hundred dollars to Stills Distributors under the name of Ritchie's Plumbing. When accounting brought him the invoice with the check, he approved the payment, coded it to Repairs and Maintenance, and waited for the check to arrive at the PO Box he had rented. Once the check arrived, Dave then went into the files one evening after everyone had gone home and destroyed any paper record of the invoice. He was over five thousand dollars richer, and no one seemed to notice.

For the next two years Dave submitted monthly invoices in various company names with various addresses. Sometimes the invoices were fairly substantial but always within reason so it would not raise any flags about the expenses. In that time frame, Dave had managed to siphon off close to a half million dollars. That amount, coupled with his regular savings, gave him just under one million dollars, which he thought he could live on with no problem. But a problem did arise.

When Dave had his retirement party at the company, it was well attended by the employees. The new CFO, Jack Williams, had been with the company for two years and studied under Dave for the last month. He was ready to take over and seemed like a capable and energetic individual. Things seemed to go well for all concerned until Dave got the phone call from Jack about three months ago.

"Dave, this is Jack Williams," he said as Dave answered the phone.

"Hello Jack," Dave responded. "How is the job going?"

"Well, I have spent the last few months looking at expenses, trying to come up with ways to improve our bottom line," Jack indicated.

"That's the job of the CFO," Dave said as he felt his pulse rise a little.

Jack went on. "I was reconciling our repair and maintenance expenses, Dave, and on the computer printout of our payables I kept coming across invoices that had no copies in the files. I double checked the names of the vendors on the invoices and cannot find any of these companies listed in any business directory anywhere in the area."

Dave felt a rush of adrenaline and tried to calm himself. "Are you sure they were not out-of-town contractors?" he asked.

Jack went on, "Not only were they not actual companies, but the work that was invoiced was never done. I checked each branch myself and there was no work done as specified on the invoices, and no purchase orders given to any of those companies."

Dave was trying to think of a response and said, "Well, you know that old Rob, our facilities manager, could have ordered the work done and not said anything to anyone about it."

"That's not what happened," Jack replied. "He may drink a little too much but he's not totally disorganized and certainly not a thief. The other interesting thing Dave, is that our payables supervisor told me that you had to sign all payables over five thousand dollars. She remembers a few invoices that came through with your signature on them that were not co-signed by Rob. Those invoices added up to a little more than half a million dollars over a two year period."

Son of a bitch, Dave thought, as he was feeling light headed. "What are you trying to say Jack?" Dave thought if he got aggressive perhaps that would help.

"I think we both know what was going on Dave. You stole over a half million dollars from this company, and I have the information and witnesses to prove it. Are you ready to go to jail?"

Dave now felt as if the world came down on him. His heart was racing, his skin felt clammy, and he thought maybe he was going to pass out. The thought of jail and losing everything he had was too much. What would he tell Norma? She had no idea what he had done. He handled the finances and kept telling her that he was getting raises and bonuses for doing good work. What would he tell anyone? He thought of the shame, the ignominy, and of dying in prison an old man with Norma in a nursing home.

LAST WALK AT RUSSELL COVE

Jack broke the long silence, "There is a way out, Dave. One that you should consider. Each month put thirty thousand dollars cash in a briefcase and leave it at a designated area. Do that for twenty-four months and you can forget about any of this. I'll call you back in a couple of days to let you know where to leave the money or I'll see you behind bars." The phone went dead.

All Dave could think of for the next two days was an image of him being locked up behind bars. The rough conditions, the gangs of inmates that would be after him, the guards hitting him and the terrible food kept coming to mind. He also could see his wife living in some rented trailer trying to make do with the small Social Security check that came in each month. Then the dreaded thought kept coming back of Norma sitting in a dirty chair in the hall of some nursing home with no money and no friends.

Dave decided he would do as Jack asked. He thought about getting the money from his various accounts. He also began to think of ways he could get out of this situation. He thought about trying to get more money so he would have some left after the blackmail scheme was over, if it was going to be over. He also thought about leaving the area and moving somewhere else where Jack could not find him. One thought that flashed through his mind was killing his wife and hiding with his money, but that thought quickly was discarded. Dave would lie awake at night thinking about his situation. He thought about finding ways to kill Jack, but could not think of anything that would make it look like an accident. He thought about going to the meeting place and confronting Jack to see if he could talk him out of the blackmail, but knew that it would be a hopeless act. Dave didn't tell his wife about the problem he was having, as it would do nothing except upset her, and he had not figured out yet what he was going to do.

Three days later Dave received the dreaded call. "Dave, this is Jack. Listen carefully. In four days I will expect you to have a briefcase full of cash that equals thirty thousand dollars."

"I can't get that kind of money that fast," Dave responded

Jack went on as if he did not hear Dave. "Take it to the parking lot in front of the Safeway store on 53rd street. Be there at 2:30 pm. Look for a blue Ford Explorer parked in the lot with a license plate number 7Y6546Z. Go up, open the passenger door on the left driver's side and put the case in the back seat. Don't look for me, but I'll be there watching you all the time. It's a rental car so the license number and type of car will change each time. Got that? 7Y6546Z. Don't screw around and don't be late. It's your future that's on the line here. And Dave, don't think about doing anything funny as I have the file. If anything happens to me the file will go to the company president, and he will most certainly give it to the police."

"How do I know you will stop when the twenty-four payments are made?" Dave asked rather desperately.

"I'll give you the file and there are no copies."

"How do I know you are telling the truth?"

"I guess you don't," Jack went on. "But what choice do you have?"

The phone went dead.

It took Dave three days to get the money out of six of different accounts. He went to the designated parking lot and after looking around, found the SUV with the designated license plates. He walked up to the vehicle, looked around and put the brief case in the back seat as instructed. He went back to his car and sat there for a few minutes and waited to see if Jack came and got in the SUV. As he was sitting there, his cell phone rang. He flipped open the phone and before he could say anything Jack's voice came across.

"I told you not to try anything, asshole. Now get the hell out of this parking lot."

Shaken, Dave did what he was told and drove home.

The second call the next month was similar but a different vehicle in a different place at a different time. Both were in parking lots in crowded areas in town. Dave once again spent three days getting his money out of different accounts, found the SUV and deposited the money. This time he didn't wait around but left as soon as the money was in the vehicle.

The third call had come in the day before they were leaving for Russell Cove. Dave explained to Jack that there were going out of town, and he could not meet the requested date.

"Too bad. You should not plan on a trip when it's time to drop the cash," Jack Williams said.

"Look Jack, I've done everything you have asked. This trip was planned for a year. I can't change it now as it involves four other couples. I will not be at any designated place you chose in the next few days."

"You sound very sure of yourself Dave. Especially for someone who is only a one small letter away from going to jail."

"I understand that Jack. We are getting to the point that if you tell on me, I'll tell on you, so cut me some slack."

"Don't get cute, asshole. My money is all in cash and is not traceable. I know you didn't mark the bills so don't threaten me."

"All right, all right. Just let me delay this one drop. I'll be on time for the rest of them," Dave pleaded.

"Delay it one week," Jack told him. "No more, no less." He then gave Dave the instructions on where to drop the money. Dave was thinking about from which accounts to get the money, and how he could put a stop to this blackmail.

"Dave, you missed the turn!" Norma's voice rang out. "I should have been watching where we were going!"

Her sudden exclamation brought Dave out of his thoughts, and he swore to himself as he looked at the turn pass by off to the right.

"You always tell me not to give you directions when we travel. Well, now you know why I do it," Norma relayed.

She took out her purse and was putting on lipstick as Dave looked for a place to turn around. Due to the narrow road he had to drive up the coast a couple of miles before he found a place to turn around. He did a U turn and started going back toward the exit he had missed. He turned into the housing development and found his way to the rented house. Three cars were already there, and five people were standing outside talking to each other while they waited for the house to be cleaned so they could bring their bags and food and drink items into the house. Dave parked the car across the street from the rental house, and he and Norma got out of the car. Dave waved at the other people standing there ready to greet him and Norma.

CHAPTER 2

Dr. Jim Schroeder was a little pissed that he was running late. It didn't seem to matter what time was set to leave the house to go anywhere, his wife Linda just could not get ready in time. He gave up years ago trying to change her tardy habit because when he tried to push her, she became upset and then everything went downhill. Jim wanted to get to the rental house at Russell Cove ahead of at least one other couple, but now it looked like they would be the last ones there, as usual.

Jim had just entered the city limits of Sebastopol and knew it was another twenty miles or so to Russell Cove. Linda was dozing, which she usually did on trips over ten miles, and came awake as Jim stopped at a stop sign.

"That was a rather sudden stop," she remarked.

Jim ignored the comment and looked at his watch. Their relationship was one of convenience after over forty years of marriage, and they knew each other very well and what it took to start a warm relationship or a frosty one. Jim decided to make it frosty.

"I would not stop suddenly unless we were running late," he replied.

Linda knew that if she responded it would be the beginning of an argument. She really didn't want to drive up to the rental house and begin their four days of fun by being upset with Jim. She ignored the remark and started looking around at the stores in the town.

Sebastopol is a small semi-urban town located fifty miles north of San Francisco. The city incorporated in 1902 and has a population of a little less than eight thousand people. The city is located in a region that produces Gravenstein apples and has become a significant grape-growing area. The city's first known inhabitants were the Miwok and Pomo Indians. In 1850 the town was formed as a small trade center for the farmers in the surrounding area. The name Sebastopol comes from the Russian seaport of Sevastopol, which underwent a British siege in the Crimean War.

The town has some very fine shops that Linda Schroeder was looking at as she was riding along, and she also spotted a few antique stores. As she was watching out the widow she was thinking about the mood her husband had been in lately. He didn't talk much and seemed to be very preoccupied.

She desperately wanted to talk to him about what had been bothering him the last few days. He had made a visit to his former medical office and when he came home he seemed very upset.

Jim was a heart surgeon and had built a very secure practice over the years. He looked good at six foot three with a slim build and muscular frame. He had a square "American type" jaw that gave him rugged good looks. He was well known for his open-heart surgeries and had a reputation for not losing patients. About four years ago Jim suffered a major heart attack. After his recovery, he started to cut back his time in the office. His semi-retirement three years ago had been difficult on his partners and patients, but Jim was ready to try something else. He wanted to scale back and only come into the office once or twice a week. It was to the point that it was getting very difficult to make a decent income with all the medical insurance plans, and the cost of liability insurance was staggering. He had managed, however, to accumulate just over four million dollars for retirement, and they were living well.

"Will you talk to me about what's bothering you," she asked as they turned on to the Bodega Highway and headed west. "Is your heart bothering you? Is it the neighbor's dog?"

"No, it's not my heart or the neighbor's dog," Jim said. *The goddamn neighbor's dog,* he thought.

Three months ago new people had moved in next door to the Schroeder's and with them came a barking dog. The dog just didn't bark during the day, but seemed to have unlimited energy and barked most of the night. Jim had talked to the new neighbor about the noise, and the neighbor said they would try and keep the dog quiet. Nothing had changed over the last couple of weeks, so Jim had thoughts of killing the dog. He purchased a small vile of cyanide pills, thinking he might just put some in the dog's food, but had not worked up the nerve. He was afraid that the veterinarian would discover the cyanide, and the neighbor would know who had slipped the pill to the dog. He really didn't want that kind of problem. He put the pills in the bottom his small doctor's bag that he always had with him. He didn't carry much in the bag except some basic doctor's tools and once in a while a vile of prescription pills. No one ever bothered his bag so he thought no one would accidentally find the cyanide pills. He planed to dispose of them but had not yet gotten around to doing it. That was not what was bothering him, however, it was something much worse than that.

"I told you before, Linda, everything is fine. Nothing is bothering me."

"You seem so preoccupied lately. Is it something I have done?"

"No, it's nothing you have done. I just have some financial things I have to work out. I'll talk to you about it later, once I find out some more information. Let me concentrate on the road. It's getting tricky now that we're getting closer to Russell Cove."

"Jim if you will not talk to me I'm not interested in going to Russell Cove. I'm not going to pretend that everything is all right between us with our friends there. So, you can turn around and take me home."

Linda surprised herself with her statement. *Well, he can take me back*, she thought. *I need to know what's going on in that mind of his. I hope it's not another woman, but if it is, he'll go out of the divorce with nothing more that his underwear in a brown paper bag.*

Jim was a little startled that Linda would be so determined to find out what was bothering him that she would sacrifice the time at the cove. He thought for a moment, and then decided to go ahead and tell her the problem.

"All right. You know that I went into the office last week," he began. "While I was there I had a voice mail recording from my two former nurses that was rather disturbing. The message indicated that Joan and Mary were going to press charges against me. They didn't say why but let me know that they both wanted to talk to me about the situation."

"Joan and Mary, they were your surgical nurses weren't they?"

"Yes, they have been working with me for over ten years. Both are very good and very competent. I called and talked to Mary and she said that both she and Joan are saying that I did a lot of open heart surgeries that were unnecessary just to get more money before I cut back my office hours."

For a minute Linda didn't speak. "That's crazy," she said. "Why would they want to do that to you?"

"For money, I guess. If they can prove I did unnecessary surgeries and get the patients to sue me, they can make some kind of financial arrangement and get some big bucks out of the settlements."

"How can they prove anything if you didn't do anything wrong," Linda replied. "You didn't do anything wrong did you?"

"No, of course not. There are some cases that were maybe borderline that could have gone either way which can be argued, but I don't see it as a problem."

Actually, Jim thought, *there are a bunch that could have gone either way, and a few that are probably provable that should not have been done. I needed the goddamn money and who was to question the decision of a prominent surgeon.*

"Well, even if they get some lawyer to agree with them, you have insurance so why worry about it?" Linda said.

"My insurance will not cover an intentional error, it only covers malpractice if you cannot prove intent," he responded.

"What does all this mean, Jim? Is there any chance someone could prove wrongdoing and win some lawsuit because you were careless?"

"I was not careless," he responded as he started to think it was a mistake talking to her about this. "There is always a risk that some jury could see that some surgery was not necessary and rule for the prosecution. If that happens who knows how much it could cost me, us. It could be in the millions."

Neither one spoke for the next mile. Both had thoughts of having no money to live on, and perhaps Jim could even go to jail.

"How did you get involved in this?" Linda asked. "We were doing so well and you were a good surgeon, at least I thought so. How could you get yourself in a mess like this? How could you do this to the family? How could you do this to me?"

"I haven't done anything to you or the family. It's a risk you take being a doctor. I'll get out of this. I'm sorry I told you about it."

"But there must be something or they would not be thinking of bringing charges, there…"

"I don't want to discuss it anymore right now," he cut in. "Let me handle it. There is no need to say anything to anyone else here this week. I don't want anyone to know the situation. Let's put on a happy face and see if we can have a good time."

"Shit," she responded, crossed her arms and looked out the passenger side window. "Shit," she said again.

Shit is right, Jim thought. Jim didn't tell Linda but he was very worried about this situation and had talked to both Joan and Mary last week when he was in the office. He called them and asked both of them to meet him there so they could discuss the situation. Both came in at the prescribed time, walked into Jim's office and closed the door.

"I understand you are going to investigate me and possibly bring charges for unnecessary surgeries, is that right?" Jim didn't even say hello but started right off with the question.

"That's correct, Dr. Schroeder," responded Joan. "We know you did some open heart surgeries that were not needed just for extra money. We have copies of the files and examinations to prove it."

"Those files will not prove anything. You know as well as I do that sometimes a doctor does what he thinks is best for the patient, even though the x-rays and symptoms may show something else."

"I'm sure that we can find experts who will say otherwise once they see the information."

"Why are you two doing this to me? You could ruin me both financially and personally."

"Well," Mary said, "We see a way to get some extra money, which we both need. You already have yours. It seems like a good way for us to become financially independent."

"No one will get anything out of this except the lawyers," Jim explained. He then had a thought. "How much would it take to keep both of you quiet?"

"We thought you might ask us that," Joan said. "Two million dollars each, and we stop our investigation."

"I don't have that kind of money," Jim replied feeling himself becoming angry. He felt his heart start to pound in his chest and tried to tell himself to calm down. "You expect me to just drag it out of the sky?"

"Doesn't matter to us where you get it," Mary said. "We're sure you have the resources to come up with that much money. We'll give you three weeks to do it. The law suits will cost you personally a lot more than what we are asking."

Jim sat there looking at the two women. *What a fucking deal this is*, he thought. "I'll be in touch, now get the fuck out of my office."

"If we don't hear anything from you in three weeks we'll contact a malpractice lawyer and begin the process," said Mary as she and Joan walked out slamming the door behind them.

After the two women left, Jim Schroeder sat at his desk trying to get his heart to slow down. He knew that what they had told him was true. He would have a very difficult time trying to prove the surgeries were necessary. He not only would face a major trial but going through something like this would ruin his reputation and would probably ruin him financially. Giving each of them two million dollars would take a major portion of his asset base and change his way of life. He tried to think of ways to get more money out of his estate but nothing came to mind. He spent the last few days running scenarios through his mind as to what he could do. He didn't have much choice, except to come up with more money, and that seemed to be a remote possibility.

He was still thinking about how to get out of this threat as he drove up to the rental house. He saw the cars parked outside and knew everyone was unpacked and inside. He and Linda would get the small bedroom again, all because she could not get her butt going on time. *Shit.*

As did the other couples staying in the rental house, Jim met Linda in college. Both were studious types and were in a lot of classes together. Jim wanted to be a doctor most all of his life and was determined to get the grades needed to get into med school. His father was a successful executive for a large food company and had enough money to put him through college. Jim and Linda both enjoyed academic success, but she wanted to teach school and not go any further with her education than getting a teaching credential.

Jim received his acceptance to a medical school in the Midwest, and he and Linda were married shortly after graduation. She had gone to summer school so she could get her degree and credential in four years of school. They moved to the Midwest, and Jim went to school while Linda taught history in a local high school. It was a difficult four years for both of them as Jim didn't seem to have time for anything but studying. They made it through those four years then Jim was accepted at a hospital in the Los Angeles area to start work on his residency. He also began work toward his specialty, being a heart surgeon. Linda continued to teach high school in an upscale area in north Los Angeles.

Jim's specialty landed him in the Sacramento area where he built a successful practice. He opened an office where he did consultations, and it was not very long before he expanded the office to include other doctors. After a little more than ten years, he purchased an office closer to the hospital that he favored.

Linda gave up teaching and started doing a lot of volunteer work. She especially liked working as a docent in one of the museums in the area. The docent work was a challenge, and each time the museum brought in a different traveling display, Linda had to become almost an expert in whatever was on display. She was also involved in various women's clubs. Their relationship had grown into one of more convenience than of emotion as Jim was always busy with his medical career, and Linda was always doing one of her favorite activities. They never did have any children, which Linda blamed on Jim's work, and harbored some deep resentment over.

Financially they had done very well. A few years ago Jim became upset with his longtime financial advisor because he didn't think he was getting enough return on his assets. He had a friend who was looking for clients and was suppose to have a good financial mind. He hired his friend to care for his investments, and his friend had not invested wisely. For years Linda wanted Jim to get rid of his friend and get another financial planner, but Jim had resisted doing that, which cost him a lot of money. His total savings were just about what the two nurses were demanding in order to keep them from exposing his unnecessary surgeries.

CHAPTER 3

The rental house had five bedrooms and five full bathrooms. The house was on two levels with the kitchen, dining room and living room on the bottom level. There was a nice deck off the living room that overlooked the golf course. You could see the ocean from the deck, and also from three of the five bedrooms that were on the upper level. Also on the deck was an above ground Jacuzzi that was big enough for four people.

Fred and Ginger Bellows, one of the five couples who had come to Russell Cove, had one of the nicer bedrooms that was on the upper level. The room was enclosed in glass, which gave the room an excellent view of the golf course and Russell Cove.

Fred and Ginger lived just outside of Sacramento in a custom home that they had built fifteen years ago. They had met in college when Fred was a cheer leader and Ginger was a song girl. She had a great figure, was fun and always seemed to have a smile. He loved watching her jump around in college with her tight fitting sweater and short skirt. They started dating when they both were juniors. He still remembers telling his fraternity brothers George and Dave, "I can't get her out of my mind. I know she'd look great without any clothes on." Fred didn't find that out until they were married, right after they both finished college. He was not disappointed then, and still enjoys watching her undress.

Fred spent time in the Army, as did most of his friends who graduated from college about the same time. He tried going into Special Forces but could not handle the physical requirements. He enjoyed telling people who didn't know him that he was in Special Forces, but actually spent most of his time as a supply officer. He thought of himself as a trained killer, but didn't learn much in his two weeks of Special Forces training. He and Ginger were never stationed outside the U.S., but did enjoy most of their military experience.

Although they wanted several children, they could only have one daughter. Ginger had a difficult time with the delivery, and the doctor advised against having any more children. Their daughter was married and living in Denver. She had three children; the oldest was just entering her teens. They saw their grandchildren two or three times a year. Fred and Ginger's relationship had its ups and downs, but overall they were still very much in love and still enjoyed each other.

The house in which they lived was in a gated community with a golf course and a nice clubhouse. Fred and Ginger both joined the country club and took part in numerous club's activities. Both were well known and liked by many people in the complex.

Fred had made his money from land investments and had done well as the town had grown. He took advantage of both residential and commercial properties that were developed to handle the influx of people coming to live in the capital city.

About a year ago Fred came home from his weekly golf game at the country club. He had retired eight months prior to that day and wanted to talk to Ginger about an investment he learned about while he was playing with his golf partners.

"Ginger, I just learned about a great investment that I think we should make. Bill Miller and Hugh Daily told me about it, and you know those two guys know how to make big money."

Ginger was in the kitchen putting the last touches to their chicken dinner. "Fred, we are comfortable with our retirement nest egg and really don't need any more money to live comfortably. I like this house and don't need anything else right now."

"I know honey, but this is a sure thing. Bill and Hugh told me about a parcel of land just outside the city limits that is going to be developed into a planned community. The owner wants to get out now rather than waiting for the red tape of approvals. It's twelve acres, and he'll sell it for a million an acre," Fred responded.

Ginger looked up from her food preparation and said, "That's twelve million dollars. We don't have twelve million dollars. What are you thinking?"

"I know that," said Fred. "Bill, Hugh and I would split the twelve million and go in together. We do have four million that we can invest. We have the three and a half million in our portfolio and we can mortgage the house for the other half million."

Now Ginger stopped what she was doing and looked at Fred with a puzzled look. "What are you thinking? That's all the money we have. What would we live on?"

"Once the county supervisors approve the development, we estimate we could sell the twelve acres for twenty four million easy. That would double our money, and we'd have eight million dollars to our name. With that much we could do so much more and really live like millionaires," Fred related.

"I don't like it," expressed Ginger. "How do you know the supervisors will approve the land deal, and when do you think that would happen?"

"It's a sure thing. Hugh told me he has talked to some of the supervisors and even put some money under the table to ensure they vote right. The deal is expected to be approved in three or four months. Then another couple of months we would sell the land to a developer. It's almost a done deal."

"I've always gone along with your investment ideas," said Ginger. "But this one seems very risky. If something happens we would really be in big trouble. I think you should pass."

It took Fred all of that evening and the rest of the next day to get Ginger to go along with his idea. They sat down and figured they had enough money to live on for eight months while the deal was being put together. Fred arranged with his broker to get the money from his investments, refinanced the house, and waited for the golden goose to lay her egg. The egg came out seven months later but not from the golden goose. It came out as a lump of coal from the devil bird.

The council meeting where the proposed development would be discussed happened seven months after the three men purchased the twelve acres, just as expected. Fred and his two friends Bill and Hugh attended the meeting expecting to go out and celebrate after the development was approved. The council meeting went as scheduled with the members going through the agenda in record time. When the proposed development came up as an agenda item, all three men anticipated a quick approval of the project.

An individual attending the meeting wanted to address the

council concerning the development project. He introduced himself as a lawyer representing one of the many local Indian tribes. He went into great detail about how the tribe researched the land and found it was a former Indian burial ground. He pointed out examples of Indian artifacts on the land and wanted the land to be frozen and not developed. He explained that if the council approved the project, they would be taken to court by the Indians and there would be a long and drawn out legal battle, of which the council would lose.

Fred could not believe what he was hearing. He sat there stunned and barely heard the discussion from that point forward. He kept thinking about his investment and how he was going to lose everything if this deal did not get approved. He was jarred out of his thoughts when he heard the council approve a motion to table the vote on the development until further investigation could be done and the Indian's claim could be researched. The council agreed to bring the matter up again for discussion in an estimated ten to twelve months.

When the council meeting was concluded, Fred just sat there in his chair thinking that this could not be happening.

"Well, you win some and you lose some," his friend Hugh Daily said trying to cheer up Fred. "We can hold on for a year or two. I'm sure it will turn out to be just fine."

Fred knew that both Hugh Daily and Bill Miller had enough money that this decision was not going to hurt them nearly as much as it was he and his wife.

"I put everything I had in this deal," Fred mentioned still looking straight ahead while sitting in his chair. "I'm ruined. I'm fucked. What the hell am I going to tell Ginger? What are we going to live on?"

"Hugh and I can swing a loan to you that will get you through this situation," Bill Miller said.

"How much can you loan me?" Fred asked.

"Probably around thirty thousand each, with a very friendly interest rate," Bill said looking at Hugh who nodded his head in approval.

"What if they don't approve the project in a year?" Fred asked, almost to himself.

"We'll see what we can do to make sure this comes out in our favor," Hugh responded.

Fred finally pulled himself together and walked out to his car. Hugh and Bill wanted to know if Fred wanted to go for a beer, but Fred declined, saying he had to get home. As he was driving home he thought of several ways to break the news to Ginger, none of which was going to be easy. He knew she was going to have some questions that he could not answer. He wished to God he had never let Bill and Hugh talk him into investing in this deal. He told himself he should have been satisfied with what he had, rather than getting greedy and wanting more. As he drove into the driveway of his house he noticed how nice everything looked. He thought how lucky he had been having a great house, money to enjoy and a wonderful wife. Now all that was gone. He took a deep breath and walked through the front door and into the house.

Ginger was in the family room listening to music from the cable channel and reading her book. Fred walked in and sat down on the couch across from her. He took the remote and turned down the music. He looked at her and told her what had happened at the council meeting.

"What do you mean they found Indian artifacts on the land!" exclaimed Ginger when Fred told her the deal had gone sour. "You said it was a done deal, Fred. My God, what do we do now? How much can you sell the land for? We need some income as we're almost out of cash and our credit cards are close to being maxed out. I'm so worried that I can't sleep at night. What are we going to do?"

"Well we can't sell the land for any amount right now," Fred said sheepishly. "The Indians have it frozen because they claim it was a burial ground for one of their former tribes. The council will not touch the subject because they think they can get involved in a big lawsuit. Right now we're stuck with a bunch of land that can't be sold or developed. It's worthless to everyone except the Indians, and they don't seem to want to spend any money protecting their dead ancestors. They just don't want them to be disturbed. I talked to both Bill and Hugh and explained to them our situation, and they said they would loan me thirty thousand each. With our Social Security checks and the loan, it should help until we can figure out how to get some money from this investment. It's going to be brought up before the council again, and maybe it will be approved then."

"When?" Ginger asked.

Fred took a deep breath and said, "In about a year."

For the first time in almost thirty years Fred saw Ginger break down and cry. She sat there in the family room chair and hung her head. Fred could hear sobs and her body was shaking. The last time she cried was when she was pregnant with their second child and lost him in the third month of her pregnancy.

"Look honey", I'll figure out something, and we'll be OK. We have always made it so far, and there's no reason we can't make it now. Let's go to Russell Cove and have a good time for the next few days," Fred said, not feeling as confident as he sounded.

CHAPTER 4

Dr. Jim Schroeder moved his suitcase into the smallest of the five bedrooms. He noticed that there were already clothes on the bed and suitcases in the corner. He looked at the suitcase and the name on the tag indicated it belonged to George Mitchell. *What the hell*, he thought as he stepped out of the room and looked for George. He found him in the living room watching a couple of golfers move up the fairway.

"Why are your things in the small bedroom?" Jim asked.

"Debbie and I thought you would be late again," responded George. "As you have had the small bedroom the last two years, we thought we'd take it this time and let you and Linda enjoy a larger room."

"You don't have to do that," said Jim. "But since your things are already in that room we'll take another one. Appreciate it George, and thanks."

"Don't worry Doc, I'll get even somehow in the next few days," commented George.

George watched Jim walk back to the small room to get his suitcase. He thought to himself that Jim looked tired, and Linda seemed to be preoccupied. *Wonder what's on their minds*, he thought.

George Mitchell had grown up in a small town in the high Sierra County of northern California. He did a lot of hunting and fishing when he was a teenager, and his parents were of lower middle class. George was big boned, six foot two, with reddish hair and played every sport available in high school. He had the grades to get into college and played football the first year he was there. He made the team as a freshman and played linebacker. The second game of the year he blew out his knee and his football career was over.

George was a very likable guy and was popular with the ladies. His voice volume was as big as he was, and people said you could hear him laugh clear across campus. He met Debbie, his future wife, through one of his fraternity brothers, Dave Wheeler, who had dated her for a while but both had moved on. George was active in student government in college and was elected Student Body Vice President his senior year. He and Debbie continued dating and became engaged and planned to marry as soon as they both graduated.

George tried to enlist in the Marine Corps after college but was rejected due to the problems with his knee. George had a degree in forestry and found out that the government was not hiring any forest rangers in northern California.

After he and Debbie were married, George took what he thought was a temporary job as a salesman with a farm machinery dealer and moved to Fresno. He quickly found out that it was going to take more than a gift of gab to sell equipment to the sophisticated farmers in the California Central Valley. He learned that the tractors he was representing were only a small part of the production cycle. He also needed to understand soils, farm implements and how they interacted with each other.

He threw himself in his work and started to read everything he could about the local farming techniques. He went to farm implement schools and learned how various tractor speeds affected the throw of dirt off the disks and plows. He learned how to change angles on disks, how to adjust a three point hitch behind a tractor and how to tell the composition of soils. In two years he got to the point where farmers were starting to listen to what he had to say. In ten years farmers were coming to him for advice.

His success grew beyond the state, and implement manufacturers started to ask his advice on new products. He developed an excellent reputation as a salesman. After thirteen years with the company the management of the equipment dealership decided to promote George to sales manager. He found himself bogged down in paper work, budgets, strategic planning and listing to the problems of his four salesmen. The farmers kept coming to George, as he knew more than the salesmen about their problems. He was working sixteen-hour days and hating it. He discussed the problem with the dealer management and it was decided that George should stay a salesman for the rest of his career. That was fine with George, and he went back to what he did best.

He and Debbie had four children. All four children went to college. All were married, and three had children. George and Debbie had seven grandchildren. Two of their children lived in the Fresno area.

George and Debbie still lived on the outskirts of Fresno and had a modest house that had been large enough to raise their four children. Debbie kept a nice garden, and George stayed involved with the equipment associations that met a couple of times a month. He also was trying to improve his golf game and was having some success in growing orchids. Both he and Debbie enjoyed reading and were comfortable with their life style.

Putting four kids through college put a real drain on their finances, but they had managed to save close to a half million dollars by the time George turned sixty-five. That money, coupled with his retirement from his company and social security, gave them enough to live on and take a couple of inexpensive vacations each year. George liked to go back to the high sierra country for a week in the summer, and Debbie liked to visit her parents in the Bay Area two or three times a year. The other time away from home that they really enjoyed was the get together with the four other couples at Russell Cove. Both seemed happy with each other and their station in life. Debbie talked a lot about her grandchildren, most of whom lived within one half hour of their home.

Although Debbie had given birth to four children, she had aged well and still had an attractive figure. Her hair was natural silver and she still got second looks from men who were middle aged and older who she met on the street.

When the time came to leave for the cove, George was ready to go but Debbie had an obligation to take care of one of the grandchildren for a few more hours.

"Go ahead and go on without me, George," she told him. "The drive is not that bad, and I will get there about three hours behind you."

"I'm not sure I want you driving that distance alone," he responded.

"You want to take the sports car, and you know I really don't like riding in that car with the top down anyway. Why don't you just go ahead and enjoy the ride. I'll be along shortly."

Although George was somewhat reluctant to leave her behind, even for a few hours, he did want to drive up to Russell Cove in his red convertible with the top down. The car was one of the few things that George really wanted but knew he should not have. When he first discussed it with Debbie, she was hesitant to encourage him to purchase the car, but thought about what a great husband he was and knew he didn't spend much money on himself.

"Honey, if you really want that sports car, go ahead and purchase it. We'll manage just fine and can handle the payments," she told him.

She remembered how proud he looked when he drove up to the house in the car for the first time. She knew that he wanted to show the farmers in the area that he had been successful and could afford this kind of car.

He wanted to show his friends in Russell Cove his new car, so he agreed to go on ahead, and left, still a little worried about Debbie.

"Be sure and take your cell phone," George told his wife, "and call me when you are about an hour out."

George had been at the rental house in Russell Cove for four hours now and had not heard anything from his wife. Although he did not want to show it, he was getting worried. The road leading up to Russell Cove was filled with curves and was a two-lane road once you left Highway 101. He was sitting in chair in the living room trying to enjoy the scenery but was not concentrating on much as he was wondering why Debbie had not called him. She was going to call when she was about an hour away, letting him know she was on her way.

As he sat there, George started thinking about the first time he met Debbie. She lived in one of the women's dorms. In the early 1960's the college they attended was different than it is today. The girls either lived in a women's dorm or off campus, as there were no sororities. There were men's dorms and women's dorms, and there were strict rules about having any of the opposite sex in either dorm. The girls had to be logged in their dorm by ten o'clock at night on week nights, and no later than two in the morning on weekends. Boys could not go further in the women's dorm than the reception area. If any boy was found in a girl's room, both the boy and the girl could be expelled.

George smiled to himself as he remembered meeting Debbie when she was going with Dave Wheeler, his fraternity brother. After she and Dave quite dating, George asked her to go to a movie with him. George took Debbie to a movie with another couple on their first date. After the movie, he walked her up to the door of her dorm and expected a good night kiss. She thanked him for a nice evening, kind of started dancing around and danced right through the entrance door, which he could not enter. He stood there kind of stunned, but determined right then that she was the one for him.

He remembered going back to the fraternity and telling his friends what had happened. In those days there were only eight fraternities on campus. The total enrolment of the campus was less than thirty-five hundred students, and it seemed that everyone knew each other.

He thought of how different the college exams were in those days. Once the exam was passed out to the attendees, the professor left the room. There were no monitors to watch the students. If anyone saw any student cheating, they would write their name on a card and drop it in a box, labeled "Welfare Council." The Welfare Council was made up of eight students, each elected by the student body. The student who was accused of cheating was brought up before the Welfare Council. The accuser was kept in a separate room, and the accused never knew who put his or her name in the box. After questioning both parties, the Welfare Council had the power to find the accused guilty or innocent. If the accused was found guilty, he or she could be expelled from the school. Not really a fair system, but there was very little cheating on exams in those days. George remembered when he was a member of the Welfare Council. One of the guys that Debbie was dating was brought before the council. After questioning, the council determined that the accused was guilty, and he was expelled from the school. George often wondered if the fact that the guy was dating Debbie had an influence on his decision.

"Debbie's here," someone cried out from upstairs. George got out of his chair and walked upstairs in time to see everyone gathered around Debbie giving her hugs and kissing her cheek.

"Hi honey," George said. "How come you didn't call when you were an hour out like I asked?"

"I tried George, but I kept getting a no response signal. If you recall, our cell phones don't work up here."

"That's right, I forgot. Glad you made it OK," George said as he gave his wife a big hug.

CHAPTER 5

The last person to welcome Debbie was Tom Decker. He and his wife Pam had driven to Russell Cove from Reno where they had moved a little over a year ago. Tom was in advertising, and he and Pam had lived in Phoenix prior to moving to Reno. Pam loved the Phoenix area and had made many friends there and was involved in several volunteer groups that kept her busy. Pam was a large, full figured woman and discovered early in life that men enjoyed rubbing up against her large breasts. She really didn't mind that kind of body play and many times had instigated the contact. That was as far as it went, however, as she always pretended it was accidental and never gave any indication that she wanted the contact to go any further.

Like the four other couples, they too had been married since college, and they had moved around with the military. Tom had his degree in American Civilization that meant that his specialty was very broad. He started working after the military in auto sales but soon found he was not cut out for sales. He was offered a job with another auto dealer as their advertising manager, which he took and did enjoy. He had several career changes with various automobile dealers, the last of which was in Phoenix.

They had settled down in the Phoenix area and had been there for almost twenty years. The first few years Pam worked in a department store. She had her college degree and started as an assistant manager in women's active wear. After just a year, they moved her up to be the manager. Although she enjoyed her job, she decided that given the chance, she would rather do volunteer work with organizations that interested her. She stopped working when her son Taylor and his wife had their first child.

Pam stayed busy watching her grandchild grow up and continued her involvement in several voluntary organizations. Pam will never forget the shock she felt when Tom came home one day last year and told her he wanted to move to Reno.

"Reno!" she exclaimed, "Why Reno?"

"Reno is an expanding area," he said, "and a lot of high tech companies are moving to that area. I have been offered a job with Acron Systems as their advertising manager. Acron is a fast growing company, and the opportunities are excellent for me to make some real money."

"I think you make enough money now, Tom. I really like it here, and I like my home, being here with our family and the social circle we have developed. What's wrong with your current job?"

"I'm not going any higher with my present company, and I'm getting bored and dissatisfied," he responded. "You always make new friends easily, and there's so much to do in Reno. It's not far from Lake Tahoe, and there are many beautiful areas around Reno."

"There is also snow and cold weather in the winter," she said. "I'm too old to tromp around in the snow and shiver all winter long."

"Well, you need to get used to it," Tom demanded. "I've already accepted the job and gave notice today that I was leaving in two weeks."

Pam didn't like it one bit, but she had been a good wife to Tom over the years and finally accepted the fact they were moving. She really didn't want to stay in Phoenix without Tom, but was deeply hurt that he made this decision without her input and just assumed she would go along.

The move was a difficult one. They found a nice three-bedroom home south of Reno and moved in within four months after Tom took the job. Selling their house in Phoenix was not a problem but what was a problem was saying good-bye to her son and his family. Plus she hated to leave all the friends and contacts that she had made in the Phoenix area. Pam also not only had to handle the move and the packing, but felt responsible to find people to replace her in her volunteer work. Tom didn't seem to want to help much as he was excited about his new job and kept telling her it would be fine. Pam watched the finances, contacted the escrow companies, reviewed the contracts and when everything was ready had Tom sign in the appropriate places. Pam always handled the finances for the two of them. She kept the check books, paid the bills and knew daily what their financial situation was. Tom was busy at work and didn't pay much attention to what was happening with their money. He planned to continue to work until he was at least seventy years old and knew they had some money in the bank and that they had another five or six years of income before retirement. He was too busy developing his career and left all the financial decisions to Pam.

The first two or three weeks in Reno were not bad. It was in the fall and the weather was nice. Pam spent most of her time arranging the house, hanging pictures and organizing things. After three weeks she began exploring around the town trying to get her bearings and finding the way to some of her favorite shopping stores.

One afternoon when she was particularly bored she stopped into a large casino to see what was inside and watch the people. While she was having lunch she saw a woman win fourteen hundred quarters on a slot machine. She figured that if she won some money then lunch would be free. She sat down at a quarter machine and slipped a twenty dollar bill in the slot. She kept winning and losing for about an hour before her twenty dollars were gone. She found not only did she enjoy the thrill of playing, but also it took up some time, so she played another twenty dollars. An hour and a half later she walked out of the casino with two hundred dollars less than she had when she went in. Well, she thought, maybe tomorrow I'll get lucky.

Pam became hooked on the slot machines. She went from quarters to half dollars to dollar machines. She would start playing the machines around ten o'clock in the morning and stayed in the casino until around four o'clock before she went home to wait for her husband. About every hour she would take a break and sit at the large bar and have tomato juice or some other type of soft drink. She noticed the bartender was very friendly and kept stealing glances at her breasts. One afternoon as she was sitting at the bar he started a conversation.

"I notice you are here about every day," he mentioned as he served her a Diet Coke.

"I enjoy playing the machines," she responded.

"I have not seen you here before the last few weeks. Are you new to the area?" he asked.

"Yes, my husband and I recently moved from Phoenix, and I

really don't like Reno."

"I'm Sheldon Monroe," he said as he extended his hand. "If you would like, I get off at four o'clock and could buy you a drink and tell you all the good things about Reno."

She looked at Sheldon. He was about mid fifties and not bad looking. His bartender outfit fitted him well and there was no sign of a stomach protruding out from his vest. He was well groomed and seemed to be nice and soft-spoken.

"I'm Pam Decker," she said as she shook his hand. *It's tempting but I don't think an affair would be the wise thing to do right now,* she thought.

"That's nice of you Sheldon, but my husband probably would not approve and things are complicated enough in my life right now. I don't think it would be in my best interest, but thank you anyway."

"Well you know where I am if you change your mind," he said as he once again scanned his eyes over her body.

For the next few months she kept playing the machines, kept talking to Sheldon once in a while. She learned that he had retired from the Navy, been divorced for five years and had three children living in different parts of the states. It got to the point that he was very open about trying to get her in bed, and it kind of became a joke between them. She enjoyed his company but never wanted the relationship to get any further than talking over the bar. Once last week as she was sipping her Diet Coke, Sheldon came up to her.

"I think I can help you win some money," he said.

She looked at him suspiciously and asked, "What do you mean?"

"I generally know which machines are hitting right now and which ones are cold. Standing here behind the bar you not only get to see a lot, but get to talk to a lot of people. They let me know what the machines are doing."

"I thought all the machines were set the same, with the same odds," Pam said.

"Well, that's what they tell you, but that's not quite true."

"OK, I'm playing the dollar machines right now. Which ones are hot?"

"I'll tell you if you go to bed with me," he said.

Pam laughed and said, "I thought you would have an ulterior motive."

"Well you can't blame a guy for trying. The third dollar machine from the left on the second row as you come in the door seems to be hitting today. Might want to try it."

Pam finished her drink and walked over to the dollar machine that Sheldon spoke about. She started playing the designated machine and started winning more that she was putting in. After three hours of sitting at that machine she was ahead twelve hundred dollars. She walked back over to Sheldon and told him the news, thanked him and went home.

Feeling guilty, she didn't talk to Sheldon much over the next few weeks. She kept playing the slot machines and kept losing. She wrote checks in the casino for more money when her wallet was empty. After six months she was shocked to add up her losses and find that she had lost over a hundred and fifty thousand dollars.

Pam knew if Tom found out about the losses he would be extremely upset. She had to find a way to win the money back. The only way she could think of was to go back and ask Sheldon which machines were hitting.

"Look, Pam," Sheldon said after she asked him to tell her which machines she should be playing. "You want something, and I want something. You know the deal. Go to bed with me, and I'll lead you to the winning machines."

"What about my husband?"

"He'll never find out unless you tell him. The maid on the third floor of this hotel is a friend of mine. We can use one of the empty rooms. I have a break in twenty minutes. Come on, you'll enjoy it."

Twenty minutes later Pam let herself be lead to an empty hotel room. She tried not to think of what was happening when Sheldon took off her blouse and bra and started kissing and caressing her breasts. The sensation wasn't all that bad, and she became somewhat aroused. Sheldon took off the rest of her clothes while he was still fixated on her breasts. He then undressed and stood there naked with his hard, erect penis. He put his hand behind Pam's head and moved her head down between his legs. She hesitated at first but then took him in her mouth. She was surprised that the action aroused her even more. After a few minutes he moved her so she would be on her back on the bed and entered her. She noticed he felt much different than Tom, but it was not all that unpleasant.

Pam walked out of the casino that day with two thousand more dollars in her purse than she had when she went in. She felt good about the money, but had major guilt feelings about what she had done that morning. She knew if she wanted to keep on winning then there would be more meetings in the third floor empty rooms.

Oh, God, how did I get myself in this situation? I'm like a whore who sold her body for two thousand dollars! I'm so sorry, Tom. I promise I will get the money back someway and still be a faithful wife, at least from now on, she thought.

She knew that Sheldon could help her with winning some money, but she was not going to make it all back doing it a couple of thousand dollars a day. That would take almost a year. She needed to hit it big, and maybe Sheldon could lead her to the big win if she was more cooperative.

That's stupid. He can't tell me which machines are going to hit the jackpot, only which ones seem to be paying off at that particular time. I don't know what I'm going to do.

Tom was oblivious to what was happening but was glad to see that Pam was becoming accustomed to Reno and seemed to be happy. He did start to notice that they kept running out of normal food items and he had to run to the local market after work to get milk and other small items that Pam used to always have available. He also noticed that she was never home during the day and seemed anxious during the weekends. They didn't talk much since they moved to Reno. Tom assumed that she was busy getting new friends and looking for new volunteer opportunities. They did have a conversation a couple of days before they were scheduled to go to Russell Cove and spend some time with their old college friends. That evening after Pam had been with Sheldon, they were starting to have dinner.

"I'm thinking of investing in another property," Tom said as they sat down and started eating. "There are some nice small homes in the Tahoe area that would make a great weekend getaway."

Pam didn't say anything but started eating her salad. "I looked at one a couple of days ago, and we could get it for around three hundred thousand," Tom continued. "Of course we don't have to take that much out of our savings, say probably forty thousand for the down payment and maybe twenty or thirty for furnishings. We'd have a nice place to spend some time together in a beautiful area. It would also be a nice investment."

"I like this house fine," Pam responded. "There is no need for us go get another house and have me spend time running back and forth finding furniture and decorating walls and things. I have enough to do already."

"What do you do all day?" Tom asked.

"I shop, clean, wash, vacuum, iron, scrub and you name it," she said

"If we got another house we could hire a cleaning lady to come in and help," Tom replied. "I think I'll go down tomorrow and talk to our bank and see what they can arrange."

Pam felt her face flush and her emotions rise and she blurted out, "We don't have the goddamn money to buy another house, OK."

Tom sat there for a few moments with a shocked look on his face. "We made some money on the sale of the house in Phoenix, and last time I looked we had close to half million with our broker," he responded.

Pam decided she might as well come clean about her gambling. "I spent a lot of it in the casinos in the last six months," she said as she put down her fork and looked directly at Tom.

"You what!" Tom said

"Don't worry about it. I have the system figured out and plan to start winning it all back tomorrow," Pam said

"How much have you lost," demanded Tom

"About one hundred and fifty thousand," exclaimed Pam as she started feeling her strength go out of her body.

"One hundred and fifty thousand dollars! One hundred and fifty thousand dollars gone down the drain. Son of a bitch, Pam, what were you thinking? Do you have any idea what that does to our financial future?"

"I told you I can get it back," said Pam as she started to feel a tear well up in her eyes. "I told you I didn't want to move here. I don't have any friends and have nothing to do. I hate it here, I hate this house, and I hate everything about this place." She jumped up from the table and ran toward the bedroom as the chair she was sitting in fell backwards.

Tom sat there with a sick feeling in his stomach. A wave of guilt swept over him as he thought of the words from his wife.

I guess I did this to her, he thought, *the way I handled the whole move. I was so intent on moving I didn't take her feelings into consideration. Why didn't our broker call and warn me about the drain on our finances?*

He then remembered that when they moved they transferred their assets to the Reno office and still did not have another broker. He remembered Pam telling him that the new guy called a few times but she had not returned the call. He really didn't want to throw his marriage away after all these years. He needed to do something that would save their relationship.

Tom got up from the table and went in to where his wife was lying on the bed. She was sobbing and didn't look at him when he came in. He sat down beside her, stroked her back and said,

"I guess most of this is my fault. I dragged you up here and threw you to the wind. Tell you what, as soon as we get back from Russell Cove I'll start looking for a job in Phoenix, and we can get back to our former life. We can get some money out of this house and since I'm working for another five or six years we can make up the money that went to the casinos."

"I'm sorry Tom," Pam muttered. "I got caught up in the gambling thing, and when I started to lose so much I really tried to tell you. I really tried to win back the money."

"It's OK Pam," he relayed. "Everything will be OK."

As he sat there with her he thought, *one hundred and fifty thousand dollars, son of a bitch!*

The next morning they packed their clothes and put their things in the car. Although they were cordial to each other, both could tell that it was a little less friendly than usual. Tom wanted to get on the road as he felt things would get better once they arrived in Russell Cove.

They traveled on Interstate 80, which took them over Donner Pass; one of the most beautiful drives in all of California, if not in the country. Tom always marveled at the distance between where the Donner Party was snowed in and how far some of the men walked to find help. He kept trying to imagine walking over the mountains and hills in the snow, trying to stay alive and believing there was a house or farm just over the next ridge. It always amazed him what some people had to go through to settle this country.

Pam was not a reader in the car. Reading while riding made her car sick. She was a sleeper and could doze for hours as they went along. That was what she was doing now, as they started to come into Sacramento. Tom didn't know if Pam was actually dozing, or pretending to doze so she would not have to talk to him.

He maneuvered his way through traffic and stayed on Interstate 80 and bypassed Sacramento, California's capitol. The Interstate took him south before he reached The City. He continued south, past Davis, the town with one of the campuses of the University of California. He stayed on Interstate 80 until he passed Fairfield then turned onto Highway 12 toward Napa.

He started to relax and enjoy the ride now that they were off the Interstate and traveling rural roads. The area was pretty and Tom started to see vineyards planted along the road. They came into Bodega Bay, knowing they were only a few miles from Russell Cove.

Bodega Bay is a town on the California coast of about 1500 people. Pam woke up and noticed the restaurants along the bay and saw some of the fishing boats as they were coming in from the day's fishing trips. She was thinking about the history of the town and remembered that in the mid 1800's a Captain Stephen Smith married a Peruvian and became a Mexican citizen in order to receive a land grant. Rancho Bodega was established, and Bodega Bay was named in the late 1800's. There was an ample supply of wood in the surrounding hills, and San Francisco was growing and needing lumber for buildings. Captain Smith built the first steam-powered sawmill in California. He cut and processed the wood from the hills, then used the bay to ship his product to San Francisco. The town grew to its largest size around the turn of the century then diminished to its current population of about 1500 about sixty years ago, not including the short-time renters like this annual get-together.

Pam still felt guilty, but wanted to warm things up between Tom and her.

"Tom, I meant what I said last night. I'll try and get some of the money back before we go back to Phoenix."

"Pam, I know you mean well, but you know as well as I do that if you continue to gamble, you will just lose more money. Those casinos were not built because people win money. They exist because people lose money."

"I think I have learned which machines are hitting on a particular day. I know I can win two or three thousand dollars a day and get most of our money back."

"If you are serious about getting our money back then maybe the best thing you can do is get a job when we get back to Phoenix. You can help build up our asset base for our retirement."

Pam had not thought about getting a job, but now that Tom had mentioned it, it didn't seem like a bad idea. This way she could be making money and have a feeling she was doing something useful at the same time. She thought about contacting the department store where she used to work.

"That's a good idea," she responded. "I'll go back to the department store where I worked before. Women's active wear should not have changed much. If I can't get hired from my old company, I'm sure I can get a job at one of the many stores in the Phoenix area. I'll work until we have enough money to retire. I'll work hard, Tom"

"I know you will sweetheart, but it's not as important as our relationship, so don't worry about it. As I said before, let's just enjoy ourselves for the next few days in Russell Cove."

He continued to drive through the countryside, trying to enjoy the scenery. His thoughts were not so much on how beautiful the countryside was, but on how he was going to build up his retirement base again at his age.

CHAPTER 6

The afternoon sun was almost covered with the incoming fog as three of the couples sat in the living room talking, reading and drinking. The other two couples were getting ready to fix the first evening dinner. Generally two couples would rotate fixing dinner each night, and one couple would take care of breakfast. Lunch was on your own as everyone was out doing something around the area and usually had lunch out. This night it was George and Debbie Mitchell and Dave and Norma Wheeler fixing dinner.

"I have a tee time for 9:30 am tomorrow," Tom Decker mentioned to Fred Bellows as they were sitting in the living room with their drinks. Tom liked his vodka and soda, a drink no one else could appreciate. "It looks like just the two of us are going to play as the rest of the group wants to do something else. Did you bring enough money to cover your bet? Remember last year I took a dollar from you."

"I remember, but if you recall I gave you ten strokes, and this year will be different," responded Fred. "I'm playing now about twice a week, and my game is improving."

"You still playing in the real estate market?" Jim Schroeder asked Fred.

"I wish he wasn't," said Fred's wife Ginger Bellows, who then took a quick look at Fred as if she had said something she shouldn't have.

What kind of look was that? Jim thought. *Did he invest a little too much somewhere?*

Fred hesitated to answer as the thought of his land predicament flashed through his mind. "Not so much anymore. You can never count on what people may find on the land that you're looking at. It is better just to invest small amounts as you will not get burned if someone finds a snub-nosed leopard lizard or some other protected animal. How about you Jim, still going to the office and doing some heart surgery?"

"I really don't do any more surgeries," replied Jim Schroeder. "I go into the office a couple of times a week just to look at x-rays. When they ask I advise some of the other doctors what they should do. I still have an office there. Linda would just as soon I not go to the office but it really doesn't take much time."

"He may have already done too many surgeries," Linda Schroeder added.

"What she means is I should have quit a few years before I had my heart attack," Jim responded quickly giving Linda a dirty look.

That was an interesting response, thought Fred Bellows. *I wonder what Linda meant with that remark?*

"How do you and Pam like Reno?" Jim asked Tom Decker.

"We are having a difficult time with the weather," Tom responded. "We are so used to Phoenix and the warm climate there that we are thinking of moving back. We would like to find a place even in our old neighborhood if possible."

"I really don't like it," Pam Decker said as she turned from the window and looked at Jim. "It gets too cold in the winter, and all my friends are still in Phoenix."

I'll have to make an effort to rub up against Pam, Jim Schroeder thought as he looked at her ample figure. *It's one of the highlights of the trip.* "Well, you can always make new friends," Jim responded. "It just takes time and some effort to join clubs or go to church, or just reach out."

"Reno is also full of gambling places and gamblers. I don't enjoy being around those kind of places," said Pam Decker looking at her husband Fred and thinking about how she missed not putting dollars in the slot machines.

"Yeah, she hates it around the gambling places," Tom Decker said somewhat sarcastically as he got up to fix himself another drink.

I wonder what that was all about? thought Jim Schroeder. *Is Pam gambling too much or something?*

Jim got up from his chair and said, "I need to refill my wine glass." He went over to the kitchen, looked around to see how close they were to eating.

He asked Debbie Mitchell, "How much time before dinner?"

Debbie looked around and studied what Norma Wheeler was doing with the salmon. "About an hour," Debbie responded as she cleaned some potatoes. "Are you hungry?"

"Yes, but, I'm thinking about getting a dollar from everyone and going down and buying a lottery ticket. Tonight is the drawing and we need to get the ticket pretty soon or we'll be too late," Jim said.

"Here's mine," responded George Mitchell as he handed Jim a dollar bill.

"This is like sticking a dollar in the stove," Dave Wheeler said as he handed Jim his dollar.

Jim went back into the living room and got a dollar from Fred Bellows and Tom Decker. He then went out the front door on his way to purchase a lottery ticket for the group.

Other than the noise of dishes and tableware being put on the table, the house was rather quiet. While Debbie Mitchell was washing potatoes, Dave Wheeler walked behind her and let the back of his hand rub across her buttocks.

She was startled for a moment, then turned to Dave and said in a quiet voice, "That's enough of that, Dave. I don't appreciate it, and I don't think George would appreciate it either."

"Just reliving a little of the past," he responded, also in a very low voice.

"That's so far in the past I don't want to remember. I suggest you put it out of your mind also. I meant what I said, that's enough."

"OK, Debbie, no harm done. I'll be a good boy the rest of the time."

Other than the quiet conversation between Debbie Mitchell and Dave Wheeler, everyone seemed to be lost in their own thoughts as the dinner hour approached. Tom Decker was thinking about the golf game tomorrow and the one hundred and fifty thousand dollars of his floating around Reno. He had been worried about leaving his job in Reno and trying to find another one in Phoenix. Fred and Ginger Bellows were wondering where they were going to get some money to live on while they struggled with the land deal. Jim Schroeder, who was getting the lottery ticket, was wondering what the two nurses were doing with the files and if they had contacted any heart surgery patients yet. Dave Wheeler was not only thinking about Debbie Mitchell, but also where he would have to drop his next thirty thousand dollars, and George Mitchell was thinking about rubbing up against Pam Decker.

Jim returned with the lottery ticket just before dinner. He also announced that he had rented the movie, *The Birds,* which they could all watch after dinner. He could only get the movie in a VCR tape, but that was all right as they had a VCR player in the rental house.

"I got a Quick Pick with six chances," Jim related to any one who would listen. "I think the jackpot tomorrow is going to be over twenty million dollars."

"Dinner is ready," Debbie Mitchell announced. "Please get a plate and help yourself and have a seat. Barbecued salmon for tonight with a good white wine."

"What's the wine?" Jim asked, considering himself somewhat of a wine connoisseur.

"Sonoma Cutrer," Dave Wheeler responded. "It's one of my favorite chardonnays."

"I'll second that," Fred Bellows chimed in. "I hope you brought enough."

The group lined up to fill their plates as the food was on the serving counter. Dave Wheeler maneuvered himself so he was in front of Pam. As they started to move through the line, Dave moved back slightly, and his upper right arm touched Pam's left breast. He could feel the softness of her breast against him and took a moment before he moved on. Pam didn't seem to notice and said nothing. When Dave turned with his full plate and looked for a place to sit at the table, he noticed George Mitchell looking at him with a slight grin on his face. Dave also noticed that Debbie had made sure that she was across the table from him so he would not be close.

The dinner conversations generally centered on what each couple was going to do the next day. They all knew that politics and the war were not subjects discussed in the group. Pam and Norma were quite liberal and the rest of the group was conservative. If someone wanted to change the mood at the table, or anywhere else in the house, all they had to do was bring up the subject of crazy Democrats or stiff Republicans, or how they were lied to about getting in the war. These subjects were not discussed.

The conversation turned to what books they had read and what they thought about them.

"I'm reading *Water for Elephants*, by Sara Gruen," Norma Wheeler said. "It's a book about the circus in the early days and is very interesting."

"I'm a W. E. B. Griffin fan," chimed in Dave Wheeler. "He's written over forty books, and I think I've read all of them. I'm reading *The Shooters* right now. That's his latest book in his Presidential Agent series."

"Jon Krakauer has a book out called *Under the Banner of Heaven*," said Jim Schroeder. "It's about the Mormon religion and is rather fascinating."

"Well, I just read something a little different. It's a management book called *Don't be a Dead Fish* and is written for individuals who are new in management or want to get into management," George Mitchell said.

"Why are you reading that kind of book?" Tom Decker asked.

"I bought it for my son, who has just been promoted to training manager in his company. I think he'll get a lot out of the book, and it will help him in his career. It will also assist him with his training responsibilities," George responded.

"Not a bad idea," Tom Decker said.

"George, what are you and Debbie doing tomorrow?" Dave Wheeler asked.

"I think we're going into town and do some antiquing. Pam, since Tom is playing golf, would you like to join us?" He then looked at Ginger Bellows and said, "Ginger, the same holds for you."

"I'd like that," said Pam Decker. George smiled thinking of being around Pam all day.

"I think I'm going to go wine tasting with Dave and Norma," answered Ginger Bellows.

"Linda and I will go wine tasting with you guys," said Jim Schroeder. "You can never get enough good wine from this area, and we might as well take advantage of it."

Dave Wheeler brought to the table his new toy, which was an electric wine chiller. The wine was already chilled. "This wine chiller will keep one bottle of wine nice and chilled while we drink the others," Dave said. "I found a long extension cord but I think it's too long to use because somebody will probably trip over it, so we'll leave the chiller on the counter and pull the wine out as we need it."

"That's a neat device," Fred Bellows commented. "How long does it take to chill the wine when it is not already cold?"

"Depending on how warm it is, it takes up to an hour to chill," responded Dave. "But it's nice to have to keep the wine chilled at the table."

"Have we decided what we are going to do with the money we're going to win tomorrow?" Jim Schroeder asked, directing his question to the group rather than any one individual.

"I have not given it much thought," expressed Dave Wheeler. "We have this conversation each year, and all we've won is a couple of bucks. I don't think it is worth talking about. Let's talk about something else; something that is close to our hearts. How about how lucky we are to have each other as friends?"

Pam Decker chimed in, "I was just thinking about that George. We've all been friends for so long. Plus we've all been married to the same people since college. That's really rare."

"We couldn't get divorced because of the kids," said George Mitchell. "Neither Debbie or I wanted custody."

Everyone laughed at George's joke.

"But really," added Debbie. "We all are so lucky to have each other. I'm sure we would do almost anything for each other. It's great to have friends like you guys."

"Let's change the subject before we all get too maudlin," Dave Wheeler said. "Is it going to rain tomorrow?"

The conversation continued about the weather and other safe subjects until everyone was finished and took their dishes to the sink. Dave Wheeler and George Mitchell had the washing duty. After the dishes were put away, they all settled down in the living room to watch the movie, *The Birds,* that Jim Schroeder had rented.

For the first hour, most everyone was quiet. They were watching the movie, and trying to identify places around Bodega Bay that they recognized. After about sixty minutes, four of the couples were lost in their own thoughts about the financial situation they were in. They didn't concentrate on the movie. As the movie approached its end, some of the couples started to go to bed.

"Doesn't anyone want anything to drink?" Dave Wheeler said.

LAST WALK AT RUSSELL COVE

"I'm going to bed," Jim Schroeder responded. "Dave you can rewind the movie for me, and I'll take it back to the video store tomorrow."

Four of the couples went to bed. Dave and Norma Wheeler stayed until the end. When the movie finished, Dave rewound the tape on the VCR, took it out of the machine and took it to his bedroom. He put it on the dresser thinking he would give it back to Jim tomorrow to be returned.

CHAPTER 7

Dave and Norma Wheeler were getting ready for bed when Norma said, "Fred and Ginger seem to have it all together. They are talking about buying another house. I think I would like to have something up in the mountains, like a cabin or condo, where we could go for a weekend. Do you think that's possible?"

"No, I don't think that's a good idea on how to spend our money," Dave answered.

"I have not checked lately, Dave, but how much do we have in savings and all?" asked Norma.

Dave hesitated for a moment. *I guess this is as good a time as ever to bring her into my problems,* he thought. *This is not going to be fun.*

"Norma, do you remember all the times in the last five or six years that I was working I told you I was getting bonus money?"

"Yes, the company was very good to you," she replied.

"Well, it really was not bonus money. I knew I would not have enough to retire on so I started sending the company false invoices. Most of that money was really embezzled."

"What?" she said.

"I put in fake invoices under several different names, got paid and destroyed the copies of the invoices. I figured no one would ever figure it out."

"How could you do that? Isn't that against the law? You could go to jail."

"I did it for us. I did it so we could have a nice life style in retirement."

"Where did you put the money?" she asked.

"I opened several bank accounts and saving accounts under

different company names, some in my name. I spent most of my time at work figuring out where and how to put the money so the IRS would not find out or be suspicious."

"How much money are you talking about?" she asked.

"Close to half our savings," he responded. "About a half million dollars."

"My God, Dave, if anyone finds out, you could go to jail, and I would be left with nothing! My God, Dave."

He looked at her, then looked away and said, "Someone did find out, and he's blackmailing me to the tune of thirty thousand dollar a month. If I don't pay him he will turn me in. I'll go to jail. By the time he's finished, or he says he's finished, we'll be down to almost nothing in our accounts."

"Who is it?" she asked.

"Jack Williams, the guy who took my place."

"How is he doing this? What does he ask you to do?"

"I have to take a briefcase with the money to a designated parking lot and put it in a designated car."

"How many have you paid?" she asked.

"Two so far," he responded.

"How many people know about this?" Norma asked.

"As far as I know Williams hasn't told anyone else. He would have to keep it to himself because of the blackmail situation."

Norma sat there on the bed for a few moments, staring straight ahead. Her thoughts went to what life would be like if their savings were gone. She thought of all the things she had purchased and collected over the years. She thought about the nice house that she worked on to make comfortable. She thought of how life would be without Dave doing things for her. She thought about not being able to afford a nice retirement assisted living facility. She thought about sitting in the hall in a run down nursing home without any money.

She rolled her eyes up and down and finally said, "Kill him."

"What?" Dave responded.

"Why don't you find a way to kill him? I'm not ready to give up all I have and live destitute because some asshole wants to take our money from us."

Dave was a little shocked at Norma's outburst. "That may be more difficult than you think. I'd have to find a way to do that and not get caught."

"I just read a story in my last book that told about a killer that would break into the victim's garage and wait until morning and shoot the guy when he came out to go to work. He put a plastic bottle over the gun barrel, and it didn't make much noise. This way you don't have to break into anyone's house, just the garage. You have to do something Dave. My God, what a situation you got us in."

"Well if I had not stolen the money, we wouldn't be living like we are. I really did it for you."

"Don't go and blame this on me. You got us into this mess, now get us out of it!" she responded.

Nothing else was said as they both completed their preparation for bed. There was obvious tension in the air, and both turned their backs to each other once they were in under the covers.

That was easier than I thought it would be, Dave lay there thinking as he listened to the distant foghorn. *Maybe I can kill him. I just need to keep thinking of ways to do it and get away with it*. His last thought before he went to sleep was how to kill Jack Williams.

CHAPTER 8

The next morning the sun was trying to break through the fog when Norma Wheeler started to make the coffee. There were lots to choose from for breakfast, and individuals started to come down to the kitchen and stand around trying to wake up. Dave Wheeler and George Mitchell left to go get a paper as Jim and Linda Schroeder came into the room.

"What time will you be ready to go wine tasting?" Jim asked Ginger Bellows as she was getting some coffee.

"Whenever you and Linda are ready, I'll be ready. I don't think you can get into most of the wineries until ten o'clock so there's no big rush to get out of here."

"Where are you going antiquing?" Ginger Bellows asked Debbie Mitchell as she came in the kitchen for some coffee.

"Probably start in Sebastopol," responded Debbie. "There are some good places in Petaluma also."

Tom and Pam Decker walked in the kitchen and went straight for the coffee machine.

"Great day for golf," said Fred Bellows. "Tom, did you bring your clubs or are you going to rent them?"

"I brought mine along," Tom Decker answered. "What time shall we go down to the pro shop to get checked in?"

"Since it's real close, how about nine o'clock. That should give us plenty of time. We'll take my car," said Fred.

"Don't forget about our walk this morning," said Debbie Mitchell.

A few minutes later as they were sitting around the table making small talk, Dave Wheeler and George Mitchell came through the door.

"You all are not going to believe this!" exclaimed George. "We hit the jackpot and won twenty one million dollars in the lottery!"

"Yeah, right," said Fred Bellows "And my dick is three feet long."

"Fred!" said his wife Ginger. "Don't talk that way."

"I'm not kidding," George continued. "We checked the paper and the numbers several times, and we have the winning numbers. Honest to God."

"He's not kidding," Dave Wheeler said. "It's right here in black and white. We actually did it. Twenty one million dollars to be split between us."

The room fell silent. Several thoughts were running through each individual's head as they contemplated what had happened. All of the couples except George and Debbie Mitchell were thinking of money to live on and getting out of a financial crisis.

"This is wonderful. How much is that for each of us?" Linda Schroeder asked.

"Well," Dave Wheeler said, "As far as I know without doing some serious checking, if you want to cash out your winnings and take a lump sum, that would equal about half the amount. You can do that or take annual installments for the next twenty-six years. I prefer the cash settlement. Then the tax man will take another forty-five percent or so, which means you will get roughly one half for cash, and one half of what's left after taxes."

George Mitchell chimed in, "I already did some figuring and this lottery ticket would mean a little over a million dollars per couple, assuming there were no other winners besides us."

"How will we find out if there were any other winners?" asked Linda Schroeder.

"We will not know until we read about it in the paper tomorrow," replied Dave Wheeler.

Pam Decker started jumping up and down, laughing and clapping her hands.

"Tom," she exclaimed, "we can move back to Phoenix and you can retire! This is just wonderful news." *And my gambling dept and Sheldon problems will be solved. Too bad I didn't know this yesterday or I would not have said anything to Tom about my problem. Thank God I didn't tell him about Sheldon,* she thought.

She ran over to her husband Tom and wrapped her arms around

him and kept laughing and making high squeaky noises.

Debbie Mitchell felt like doing the same. "George, that's great for us too. We can have some money now to help the kids and not have to worry about it."

"We brought some champagne back, does anyone want any this morning?" asked Dave.

"I wanted to run the ticket through the lottery machine at the store to verify our winnings, but Dave was against doing that and said we should discuss it with the group before we verify anything," George Mitchell said.

"I didn't want the world to know we won yet," responded Dave. "Who knows who would contact us and how many people would realize we won. We may want to think about how we are going to announce our winnings to the world."

"I don't see any problem with that," George mentioned. "What's wrong with people knowing that all five of us went in together and won the twenty-one million? We are going to have to do it sooner or later."

The same thought went through Fred Bellows' and Jim Schroeder's mind that Dave Wheeler had earlier: *What if we only split it one or two ways rather than five?*

"Let's just keep this quiet for a couple of days and let us think about this newfound money," Fred Bellows said. "There is no real rush to tell everyone about this. Let's not do something rash that we'll regret later. Let's not even tell our families yet."

Everyone except George Mitchell and Tom Decker agreed. "It still does not make sense to me," George mentioned. "But if that's what the group wants to do, then I guess Debbie and I will go along with it."

"I guess we will too," Tom said, trying to keep his balance with his wife Pam hanging on him.

"What great news," Ginger Bellows said, thinking of having enough money now to at least live on awhile and wait for the land deal to get approved by the council.

"Come on Tom," Fred said. "Let's go play some golf." Fred Bellows got a smile on his face and said, "We can afford it now. In fact we can afford a lot of things. You want to bring your clubs or buy new ones when we get to the course?"

"You two go ahead and have your golf game," Dave Wheeler said. The rest of us will do what we had planned and get together this afternoon before dinner and discuss how we are going to handle the lottery situation. I'll put the ticket in my room in a safe place and let each of you know where it is."

"I don't think it should be left in the room," Jim Schroeder said. Put it in your wallet Dave, and keep it close to you all of the time."

"Yeah you're right," Dave Wheeler said as he put the ticket in his wallet. "Enjoy the day as it will be a good one for all of us."

The rest of the group that was not playing golf went back to their rooms and put on their walking shoes. They gathered again at the front door and discussed which way they were going. If they went to the left, they would go up a slow incline, down a steep hill, then go along a flat area and get back to the house in a long slow incline. Obviously going to the right would be opposite, starting out with the long slow decline, ending up with a decline back to the house after the steep uphill climb.

They decided to go to the right, as most of them thought walking up the steep hill was better exercise. They all started walking together and then slowly broke into pairs. Generally it was natural that the guys walked together as did the girls.

As Debbie Mitchell walked along with Norma Wheeler, she started talking about what she was going to do with the money that they have won.

"The first thing I'm going to do is replace all the carpet in the house," Debbie said. "I might put the living room and dining room in a nice wood. What are you going to do with the money Norma?"

"What?" Norma said. She was thinking about what her husband Dave Wheeler had told her last night about Jack Williams and the blackmail scheme. "I think I will do the same. We could use some new carpet in the house."

Debbie continued to talk about doing things to the house as Norma, once again, tuned out. She could not think of anything else except what Dave had told her.

I think we can get by with the million dollars even after we pay off Jack Williams. But what if he learns about our winnings and wants more money? Norma Wheeler thought.

George Mitchell was having the same trouble with Dave Wheeler as they walked.

"A million dollars will bring you some real financial security," George said as he smiled. "You can live a long time on a million dollars if you invest it right."

"You can go through a million dollars pretty fast if you're not careful," said Dave Wheeler.

"I'm sure we're going to spend some fixing up the house, but the majority of it will go into retirement savings," George continued. "Maybe we'll give some to our kids for a nice Christmas gift," he continued.

As Dave Wheeler was walking along he was watching the road and noticed how it curved around in a large circle. The steep hill they were starting to walk up had a twenty to forty foot drop off on the left side as they were walking against the traffic. Both he and George walked on in relative silence, both lost in their own thoughts.

Linda Schroeder and Ginger Bellows were walking together and both were surprisingly quiet for two women walking. Both were thinking about the money they had won and how it would help their situation. Linda Schroeder was thinking about how the million dollars would go toward the potential law suits or blackmails, and Ginger was thinking about how long they could live on the million dollars and if they could last until the land was sold.

If we pay those nurses four million dollars, Linda Schroeder thought, *then that leaves us with only a little over a million to live on. Can we live on a million dollars for the next fifteen or twenty years?*

Ginger Bellows was thinking along the same lines. *A million dollars will get us out of debt and repay Fred's friends. I don't know how much we'll have left over but it's going to be better than what we have now.*

Jim Schroeder had teamed up with Pam Decker. He was telling her how important it was for him to take long walks due to his heart problems. Pam Decker was so happy she was almost skipping up the hill. Jim noticed how her breasts bounced as she moved along. The conversation eventually got around to living in Reno, and Pam opened up a little more than she had last night.

"I really don't like living in Reno," she said. "Tom has told me that he was sorry that he took this job in Reno. He said we can move back to Phoenix. Winning the million dollars will sure make that decision easier for us now. We probably will not get much out of the house in Reno as we have not been in it very long. But that's not such an important matter right now."

"Don't you have a son living in Phoenix?" asked Jim.

"Yes, Taylor, lives there with his wife and one daughter. I miss seeing them and the little one will be real happy that Granddad and Grandmother are coming back. How is your health Jim?"

"I'm trying to take good care of myself. It seems if I take a nice long walk about every other day I feel better. I haven't had any unusual heart beats now for a couple of years."

"Did getting out of the office help?" Pam asked.

"I don't think it much mattered, but you will never convince Linda of that."

The walk concluded after about an hour and everyone changed their clothes and left for their respective activities, saying they would see each other later that afternoon.

CHAPTER 9

Fred Bellows and Tom Decker were lost in their thoughts as they loaded the car and prepared to make the short drive to the golf course. The Ocean View Golf Course is a beautiful course that winds its way through some of the rental housing development then through hills with no houses in sight. There is a view of the ocean from almost every hole. It has a course slope of 127 if played from the blue tees, which means it can be difficult and challenging. Fred and Tom noticed that the course was virtually vacant as they checked in with the pro shop.

"The name is Bellows, and we have a have a 9:30 tee time for a twosome," Fred said to the golf pro who was checking them in at the Pro Shop. "It doesn't look to be very crowded today."

"No, you will have the course almost to yourself, Mr. Bellows," the Pro responded. "There is a twosome going out a little after you two, but that's about it for the next hour or so."

That will be just fine, Fred Bellows thought, as a plan was developing in his head.

Nothing wrong with that, Tom reflected to himself as he thought about the lottery money.

The twosome paid the green fees, walked back down the short path to the carts and started to load their clubs on the cart.

"You want to drive?" Tom said to Fred. "You have played here more than I have and probably know the course better."

"Sure," responded Fred. "The bets the same? Quarter a hole for skins?"

"You got it."

They spun a golf tee to see who would be the first to tee off and the tee pointed to Tom. He stepped up and looked over the first hole. It was fairly level but had a deep ditch you had to go over to reach the fairway. The ball had to travel about one hundred yards just to reach the fairway. Tom hit his drive and the ball went straight and just bounced up on the back edge of the fairway.

"Nice shot," Fred said. "At least you made the fairway. This first hole is an intimidating SOB." Fred then hit his drive straight out about two hundred yards in the middle of the fairway.

"Nice shot yourself, asshole," Tom said with a smile on his face.

As each man hit their shots and made good and bad comments back and forth, each were thinking about the lottery money. Tom Decker was very happy about the fact that he could now easily move back to Phoenix and not worry about a job for awhile. He thought that once Pam returned to her favorite city, things would settle down, and they would get back to what he considered normal times. Not only that but they would be close to their son and family, and that would make everyone happy. He still got a little pissed each time he thought of his wife losing half of his savings, but now it really didn't matter.

Fred Bellows, on the other hand, was thinking that he needed more than his one-fifth share of the lottery. He kept thinking of how he could get the money and his only conclusion was to try and eliminate some of the other couples that were his good friends. It was not a very pleasant thought, but he believed it has to be done for his and Ginger's well-being.

When you get right down to it, the name of the game is survival of the fittest, he was thinking. *I just have to devise a way to make things happen and make them look like an accident.*

As they moved down the golf course, talking and kidding each other, Fred was starting to put a plan together. By the fourth hole, Fred thought he had a failsafe way of completing the first phase of his plan.

Fred was thinking about what he was about to do. His golf game was not going well, and Tom noticed.

"What do you have on your mind, Fred?" Tom asked. "I'm already six strokes ahead of you. That's very unusual for your game."

"I guess I'm thinking of the lottery money, or something else," he responded, trying to sound relaxed. Fred could already feel his heart rate getting faster. *I hope I have the strength to do this,* he thought. *I have to keep thinking of Ginger. I have to get my mind around the fact we need the money.*

As they rode to the next hole, Fred Bellows noticed a twosome coming up behind them. The sixth hole was a par three. Since Tom was scoring better than Fred, he teed off first. His ball went straight and landed about twenty yards short of the green. As Fred started to place the ball on the tee he said, "When we finish this hole, let's let that twosome behind us play through on the next hole. We're out here to have a good time and not to be rushed."

"Sounds good to me," Tom responded.

"Are you still buying and selling real estate?" Tom asked Fred.

"The market is terrible right now," Fred responded. "I think it's going to be a long while before it comes back. We've got some money tied up in some land that we can't sell or move due to permit problems. Why are you and Pam moving back to Phoenix so soon?"

"Pam hates Reno," Tom responded.

I've got to win this hole, thought Fred. *It's important that I hit my ball first on the next hole.*

Fred tried to concentrate on his shot from the tee. He hit a good shot that landed about ten feet from the pin.

"Great shot, Fred," Tom said. "Looks like whatever was bothering you is gone."

Tom muffed his second shot and ended up with a four on the hole. Fred double putted but still had a par.

After playing the hole, Fred and Tom walked up to the tee on hole number seven. Holes number seven and eight were out of the rental housing area and built into the rolling hills. Hole number seven was 377 yards from the tee to the green, and was the most difficult hole on the course. The green was a little higher than the tee but between them was a steep valley that sloped from right to left. The cart path took a steep downward incline to the bottom of the valley before it started up again toward the green. Just as the cart path started up to the green, a large sand bunker was placed there to catch any golf balls that did not stay on the slope of the hill. There was about a twenty foot drop-off on the left side of the cart path as it went down the hill. Fred and Tom decided to wait for the twosome behind them to come up to the tee.

The two golfers who were behind Fred and Tom rolled up to the seventh tee in their cart.

"We decided to let you guys go through," said Fred.

"OK, if that's what you want us to do," responded one of the players in the cart.

"It's a nice day, and we just want to relax and take our time," Tom said.

The two golfers stepped up to the tee and took their turn hitting their ball with their drivers. Both had good shots and neither ball rolled into the sand bunker at the bottom of the hill.

"Take your time, gentlemen," Fred said as the two men got into their carts and started down the hill.

"Let's wait until they are off the green," Fred continued. He knew that once the golfers were off the green and headed toward the next hole they would be out of sight but not out of hearing range.

As they waited for the two gentlemen to finish the hole, Tom continued to talk.

"You know, this lottery win is really great for Pam and me. It solves a lot of problems, and makes the move back to Phoenix much easier."

"That's nice," Fred said, trying to keep his heart from beating out of his chest.

"Money is nice," continued Tom. "But the really great thing in life are friends. Pam and I are really lucky to have friends like you and Ginger. Thanks for being our friends for all these years."

God damn it Tom, you are not making this any easier, thought Fred.

After about ten minutes the two golfers finished their putts, went to the cart and started for the next hole. Fred stepped up to the tee, took a practice swing, approached the ball and then stepped back.

I have to do this, he thought. *God give me the strength to carry this through.*

Hs heart was now racing like crazy. He could feel his hands getting sweaty. He took a couple more practice swings, stepped back from the ball and stood behind it. He looked down the fairway like he was concentrating on his shot.

"You going to hit the ball or just watch the fairway?" Tom said.

Fred took a big breath that filled his lungs. He took a half step toward Tom and swung the club head high. Tom saw the club coming and tried to swing his head out of the way. He was not fast enough, and the club caught Tom in the side of the head at a glancing blow. Tom dropped to the ground like a rag doll.

Sorry old buddy but money is my priority right now, Fred thought. Fred quickly looked around and could not see another living soul anywhere. He got both his arms and put them under Tom and brought him to a half sitting position in his lap. About this time Tom was starting to regain consciousness. Fred then put one hand under Tom's chin and put the other hand on the back of Tom's head. Tom started to resist a little as he realized what had happened. Fred closed his eyes, took a deep breath and gave Tom's head a hard twist with both hands. He heard a "snap" as Tom's neck broke. Fred sat there a minute with his dead friend in his lap. His heart was still racing. He felt a tear trickle down his cheek. He tried to gather his thoughts and once again convinced himself that he had done the only thing he could.

Fred pushed Tom's body away from his lap and let it lay on the ground. He stood up and once again looked around. There were still no other golfers in sight. He walked a few feet toward the last hole to look at the houses he could see from the tee box. He could not see anyone out in their yard or around their houses. Once again he took a deep breath and walked back to where Tom lay.

He dragged Tom's body to the cart and with a lot of effort, sat the body in the cart on the driver's side. He positioned the cart on the path so it would travel down the cart path to the bottom of the hill. He put the cover back on his driver and put it in the golf bag. He picked up his seven iron, his pitching wedge and his putter and put them on the ground.

He went back to the tee and picked up Tom's driver that Tom had dropped when he was hit with Fred's club. He made sure he used his gloved hand to carry the driver back to the cart. He also picked up Tom's golf ball and tee that Tom was going to use for his tee shot and put them in his pocket. Fred then wedged Tom's driver between the seat and the accelerator pedal with his gloved hand and the cart started down the hill. Fred quickly jumped out of the way, picked up his three clubs and started running through the fairway on the upper right side of the hill.

Fred got about fifty yards up the fairway when he looked over and saw the cart disappear over the edge of the hill. There was some noise as the cart hit some scrub brush and it tipped over as it rolled down the hill. Fred took his golf ball and threw it as far as he could in front of him making sure it stayed on the upper side of the fairway. He took Tom's ball he had in his pocket and threw it toward the sand bunker that was next to the cart path at the bottom of the fairway and watched the ball roll into the bunker. He took a deep breath and yelled, "Tom …Tom, are you OK? Tom, Oh my God, Tom what happened?"

Fred waited for a few seconds until he saw the top of the head of one of the golfers that had played through start to appear over the horizon. He started running down the fairway toward where the cart had run off the cart path, knowing that he now had a witness that saw he was not near the cart as it went over the bank of the hill. Fred kept yelling Tom's name as he approached the area where the cart rolled off the cart path. He dropped his clubs and started down toward the overturned cart. When he reached the cart he quickly looked for the golf club that had been wedged on the accelerator and noticed it had been knocked loose. Most of the golf clubs had been thrown from their bag and Fred placed the driver next to some of the other clubs that were lying on the ground. He waited for about fifteen seconds, then located his cell phone, flipped it open and saw the "no service" indicator, which he expected to see. He went back up to the cart path and started yelling,

"I need help down here. My friend's been hurt bad, and my cell phone doesn't work. Somebody call 911."

As expected, the two golfers that had gone ahead of him were both standing on top of the horizon close to the next tee box. One of them disappeared from view and the other one yelled down,

"We'll call 911 for you and be right down to help."

Fred went back to the overturned cart and surveyed the area. Tom's body was lying about twenty feet from the cart. It appeared to Fred that it looked like he had been thrown out and had broken his neck. He reached down and put his fingers on Tom's neck and then on his wrists acting like he was checking for a pulse. *Things are going as expected*, he thought. *Now I just have to convince everyone it was an accident, which should not be a problem.*

The two golfers showed up in their cart.

"I called 911, and the ambulance and fire engine should be here in a few minutes. How is your friend, and how can we help?"

"He's dead," responded Fred. He was sitting on the edge of the cart path with his head in his hands.

"Are you sure?" asked one of the golfers. "How did it happen?"

"As you know we waited until you two cleared the green before we teed off. I hit my ball on the upper side of the hill, and Tom put his in the bunker, here next to the cart path. I figured I was about a seven iron from the green so I took my seven iron, my pitching wedge and putter and told Tom I'd see him on the green. There was no reason to ride to the bottom of the hill in the cart then walk up the side of the fairway. As I started walking toward my ball I heard Tom start the cart and proceed down the hill toward the bunker. Then I heard a noise, turned around and saw the cart going over the side of the hill. I started yelling and started running down the hill toward the crash site and found him lying near the turned-over cart. Son-of-a-bitch, I don't have any idea what happened. Damn, what a terrible thing."

"I saw you running down the hill," one of the golfers said. "We heard you yelling as we were on the tee ready to tee off."

"I'm really glad you guys were here. I don t know what I would have done with this situation and a dead phone."

The three of them were still talking when they could hear the sirens coming up the development toward the course. The ambulance turned and came on down the cart path while the fire engine stopped at the top of the hill on the street and stayed there with all its lights blinking. The ambulance stopped just in front of where the three golfers were standing. Two paramedics jumped out and asked, "Where's the injured person?"

"He's by the cart down the hill," Fred said as he pointed to where Tom was lying. "No need to hurry because he's dead."

"How do you know he's dead?" one of the paramedics asked.

"I felt for a pulse and couldn't find one. He isn't breathing and he's not moving."

The two paramedics climbed on down the hill, stood there checking Tom's body for a minute or two and nodded their heads at each other. They then came back up the hill. "He's deceased," one of the paramedics said. "We need to call the sheriff's department as there has been a fatality. I'm afraid all three of you gentlemen will have to stay here until someone from the sheriff's office comes out and talks to you."

"Why do you need to call the sheriff if it has been determined to be an accident?" asked Fred.

"As I said, it's standard procedure when there has been a fatality," the paramedic answered.

"But you can plainly see that it was an accident!" Fred exclaimed.

"Mister, we don't have any choice in the matter. Our instructions are to call in the authorities when someone has died. There may be a few exceptions to this procedure, but this is not one of them."

Damn, I was not counting on getting the police involved in this. I guess I should have known, but there still should not be a problem as I'm sure they will determine that it was an accident, Fred thought. "Why isn't this one of the exceptions?"

The paramedic just looked at Fred without saying anything, then turned around toward the ambulance, flipped open his cell phone and voice called a pre-programmed number.

CHAPTER 10

Detective Wilt Morrison was sitting at his desk in the County Sheriff's office when the phone rang. As usual, he was chewing on an unlit cigar. He picked up the phone and answered, "Sheriff's office, Morrison here."

He listened to the paramedic tell him about an accident on the Ocean View Golf Course and that the individual driving a golf cart was killed. Wilt asked the paramedic if there were any witnesses and was told there were three individuals who saw the accident. He asked the paramedic if he had any yellow tape in the ambulance that they could use to tape off the area. The paramedic said they had some tape so Detective Morrison gave instructions to hold the witnesses there, tape off the whole area, and instruct any other golfers to skip that hole. He said he would be there in about twenty minutes, thanked him for the call and hung up the phone.

Some dumb shit drove the cart off the path and killed himself, Wilt thought. *Probably drinking too much beer.* He then logged out and walked out to his car and started driving toward the scene of the accident.

Wilt had grown up in a small town in New Mexico. He wanted to see the world and joined the Marine Corps when he was eighteen years old. His recruit training took him to San Diego, and he fell in love with the city. After basic training he was stationed at Camp Pendleton and spent every minute he could exploring and getting to know all of the areas of San Diego.

He enjoyed the Marine Corps and found that due to his hunting experience where he grew up, he had a knack for shooting. He became a Marine Sniper and waited to be deployed somewhere so he could show his talent.

Halfway through his first four-year obligation he married his high school sweetheart. He brought her to the West Coast and planned to make the military his career, have children and a happy life. He was stationed at Camp Pendleton for most of his tour of duty. He did deploy for one mission to the Far East, but it only lasted eight months and he did not see any combat. After about a year of marriage his wife became unhappy with the San Diego area as there were too many people and things were too expensive. She also hated that he was in the Marine Corps. In order to try and save his marriage, he left the Marine Corps when his tour of duty was up and looked for employment in the San Diego area. He told her she would grow to love the area, just as he had.

He was accepted into the San Diego Police Academy and became a city policeman. He found that his wife hated police work worse than she hated the Marine Corps and left him returning to New Mexico. Wilt spent the next ten years in San Diego trying to keep his life together and being a good cop.

Wilt was a rough looking man with a big boned frame. He had a well-trimmed mustache that grew under a well pronounced nose. He stood six foot one inch but seemed larger. He kept himself trim and muscular with weights and long runs. For a few years while he was in the Marine Corps, he started smoking cigars. After a doctor scared him about lung cancer, Wilt started chewing on the cigars without lighting them. It was hard to find Wilt without an unlit cigar in his mouth.

Women found him attractive, and he took advantage of the opportunities that came his way as a policeman. Although he never admitted it, his extra-marital activities contributed to his marriage problems.

A year after his divorce, he remarried a girl who was divorced from another policeman. Problems his second wife had with her first husband and his work carried over into her second marriage. She was unhappy and constantly after Wilt to quit police work and do something else. Despite the problems that Wilt was having, he proved to be an excellent policeman and was promoted to detective. He had the reputation of being consumed by his cases. Once he got on a case, he thought about it twenty-four hours a day until it was solved. Working the bars and streets of San Diego brought many temptations with women, which Wilt had a hard time overlooking.

These temptations and the long hours he was putting on the job cost him his second marriage.

Detective Wilt Morrison decided he wanted a change in scenery so he quit his job and became a policeman in the city of San Francisco. Although he had several girlfriends, he was a lonely man and started drinking.

It was during the fifth year as a cop in San Francisco that he and his partner received a call that there was a robbery in progress at a convenience store near their location. When they approached the store they noticed the perpetrator running out of the store. Wilt went after him as his partner circled the block to cut off the perpetrator from the opposite direction. As Wilt rounded a corner, he felt himself being thrown against a wall with a terrible pain coming from his right side. He tried to remain conscious as he slid down the wall into a sitting position. He could see the perpetrator a few yards in front of him with a gun in his hand. He could see flashes from the gun, and felt something hitting the side of his head. He managed to get out his pistol and fire six shots at the perpetrator before the pistol seemed to weigh a hundred pounds. He dropped the gun and passed out.

Wilt came to in the hospital. He learned later that he had been shot in the right side, just above the waist. He also learned that the perpetrator continued to shoot at him from twenty yards but missed every shot. What he felt hitting the side of his head were bits off the wall as the bullets went into it. He also learned that four of his six shots hit the perpetrator, and he was dead on the spot.

The shootout gave Wilt a bit of notoriety within the police department and after a long recovery, he was once again promoted to detective.

He started drinking again during his recovery period and began to think about how he had messed up his life. Two failed marriages, no children, and he had nothing to show for his hard work and long hours except a scar on his right side.

After a few more years of chasing killers and drug dealers, he also got tired of seeing the city get overcrowded with homeless people and beggars. He didn't like the political atmosphere of the city and began to drink more and tell everyone who would listen what he thought of the city and its problems. His co-workers started avoiding him as he was full of bitterness and foul language. His supervisor was finally fed up with Wilt's attitude and called him into his office.

He told Wilt that he was a good detective but was drinking too much and was disrupting his division. He informed Wilt that he was going to let him go but because of the good work that he had done, he would keep him on the payroll for thirty days. In that time period if Wilt could get another job, he would not tell his new employer about his problems so Wilt could leave with a clean record.

Wilt was stunned. After trying to argue with his supervisor for an hour, he turned in his gear, left the office and went back to his apartment. For the next four days Wilt stayed in his apartment, doing nothing but drinking Jack Daniel's, chewing on cigars, and thinking how he had messed up his life. He thought about suicide more than once but didn't get up the courage to do anything except continue to drink. On the fifth day he heard a knock on his apartment door and mumbled that the door was unlocked. What walked through the door changed his life.

A woman by the name of Pearl Henderson walked into Wilt's apartment. Pearl had worked with Wilt and knew what a good detective he was. Pearl had been married to a military man for thirteen years before he was killed in Iraq. That was five years ago and she had been living alone since that time. She'd taken a liking to Wilt, but never showed it at work. She was not a large woman, about five foot five, but had a solid body from exercising. She had a nice figure, large brown eyes, and hair that was well kept that just touched her shoulders. Most men considered her attractive, and she did not lack offers from the opposite sex.

She walked over to Wilt and told him to stop feeling sorry for himself and get his sorry ass in the shower. Wilt was surprised but did as he was told. Pearl poured all the Jack Daniel's she could find down the drain and started to clean up the apartment. For the next two days she worked with Wilt and got him cleaned up.

Every time he wanted a drink, she talked to him about his strengths and his values. They talked and told each other their life stories. For whatever reason, Wilt felt he had a chance to get his life in order and started to believe in himself again. He found a real affection for this woman and wanted to please her. The third day she pushed him out the door and told him to go and find a job. After a few minutes she heard a knock on the door and when she opened it, he was standing there.

"I can't just go out in the street and look for work," he said. "I have some contacts up north. I need to call them and see what's available."

She let him back in the apartment and sat him down at the phone. She sat across from him and watched him make his phone calls.

After two days of contacting other police agencies, he found a position. Concerned about living alone again and wanting Pearl to be a part of his life, he asked her to move up north with him. She agreed, quit her job, and they have been together ever since.

It was six years ago when he hired on with the North County Sheriff's department and began investigating crime north of San Francisco. Pearl went with him and found work as a receptionist and record keeper for a dental office. Wilt had not had a drink since Pearl walked through the door into his apartment, and once again he became a good investigator. Since he stayed sober, he was doing well in his current position. Pearl kept after him to get married but he didn't want that obligation just yet.

He had solved a few homicides in the last few years, but this was the first golf course accident in which he was involved. As he approached the golf course he turned on his blinking lights and followed the road until he saw the fire engine parked on the street with its lights still flashing. He parked and got out of the car, noticing two firemen standing by their truck talking. As he walked up to them one said, "Detective you can drive your car down to the accident site on the cart path."

"That's OK," he responded. "I'll walk down. If I walk I can take in the whole area where the accident happened." He then ducked under the "DO NOT CROSS" yellow tape and walked up to the tee box and studied the area. He noticed nothing unusual on the tee box and looked out over the fairway. He saw where the paramedics were standing with three other men half way down the fairway and on the left side. He noticed a golf ball down the course on the upper right side of the fairway. He studied the path as he walked down to the accident area. There were no skid marks on the cart path and as he approached the scene he could see the wheel tracks where the cart had veered off the path going down the hill.

Fred Bellows was still sitting on the cart path with his head in his hands thinking about what he had done. *I have to maintain control of myself. If this is going to work, I have to quit thinking about what I have done. I need to make myself believe it was an accident.*

"Here comes the detective," mentioned one of the other golfers.

Fred looked up and saw a large man chewing on a cigar coming towards him on the cart path.

"My name is Detective Wilt Morrison," Wilt said to the group of men as he approached them. One of the men was sitting along side the path with his head in his hands. "I'm going to look at the accident scene and will be back to talk to all of you about this."

Wilt then studied the scene from the cart path. It looked like the cart rolled off the path and flipped over once as it went down the slope before getting caught in the tall brush. Wilt noticed the cart was lying on its side and a body lying about fifteen or twenty feet from the overturned cart. The body was about five feet below the edge of the golf path. Golf clubs and other debris were spread down the hill and around the cart. He walked down to the body and studied it. The man's head was turned a strange way, and he was obviously dead. It appeared that the body was either struck by the cart as it over turned, or the man was thrown out of the cart as it rolled over. He noticed a bruise mark on the side of the man's head, where it seemed the cart had hit him. Wilt took out his camera and took several pictures. He then went back up the hill and approached the individuals who were waiting for him

"Who can tell me what happened here?"

The man sitting alongside the cart path with his head in his hands stood up and said, "I'm Fred Bellows. I was playing golf with Tom when he had this terrible accident."

Wilt got out his note pad and began taking notes. "Tell me what happened, Mr. Bellows."

"Well, the two of us were playing golf and when we came to this hole, we decided to let the two golfers behind us play through." Fred pointed to the two other men standing there beside the paramedics. "After they cleared the green I drove the ball out on the right side of the hill. Tom…"

LAST WALK AT RUSSELL COVE

"What is the individual's full name?" Detective Morrison interrupted.

"Tom Decker," Fred responded.

"Go ahead, Mr. Bellows."

"Tom put his ball on the tee and hit his drive straight down the fairway but it had a slight hook. It landed in the fairway then rolled into the sand bunker right here," Fred said as he pointed to the bunker next to the cart path. Detective Morrison walked over and noticed a golf ball lying in the sand bunker.

"I figured I was about a hundred and sixty or seventy yards from the green so I took my seven iron, pitching wedge and putter and started walking toward my ball. There was no reason to ride down the hill with Tom because I would have to walk up the hill to my ball. I started walking as Tom was putting his clubs back in his bag. I heard the cart start down the hill but didn't pay any attention until I heard the noise of the cart going over the hill. I yelled Tom's name, and when I didn't get a response I ran down here and found him lying there as you see him now. I checked his pulse and didn't feel anything so I got my cell phone out of my golf bag and started to call 911. I noticed my phone didn't have any signal so I went back up the hill and saw the two golfers who were ahead of us standing on the top of the hill looking down and me. I yelled at them to call 911 and then sat down to wait for the ambulance."

Detective Morrison again looked at the fairway and saw three golf clubs lying by the side of the sand bunker. He then turned to the two other men standing there.

"Which one of you called 911, and what did you see?"

"I'm Richard Bolton, officer, and I called 911. I was at the tee box on the next hole when I heard someone yelling. I walked over to the edge and looked down and saw this man running down the hill toward the cart path. I didn't see the golf cart anywhere and wondered what happened. This man (pointing to Fred Bellows) disappeared over the hill for a few minutes, then came up and yelled up to us that his friend had been hurt and please call 911. My cell phone works fine up here so I put in a call to the fire station."

The other individual who was standing there said, "I'm Mike Freedman. I was playing a round with Richard when this all happened. I saw Richard call 911 then come back to tee box. He told me there was an accident, and we should go back and see what we could do. We came down here, found the accident scene, and waited for the paramedics to arrive."

"Where are you two from?" Detective Morrison asked the golfers.

"We both live in Sebastopol," Richard Bolton answered.

"Mr. Bellows, where are you from, and where is the accident victim from?"

Fred explained that he lived in Sacramento and Tom Decker lived in Reno. He told Detective Morrison about the five couples and how they come up once a year and rent a house. He went on about all of them knowing each other in college and how they have been friends since college.

"Do you know of any health or mental problems that your friend had?" asked Detective Morrison.

"I think I know, or knew him pretty well and was not aware of any problems of any kind."

"You said there were five couples that came up here. Where is, uh, Tom's wife?" Detective Morrison asked as he referred to his note pad looking for Tom's name.

"She is with one of the other couples looking at antiques in Sebastopol or Petaluma," responded Fred.

"Can you get in touch with her?" Detective Morrison asked.

"Once I can get to a place where my cell phone works I can."

"Give me the address of your rental house, your full name and address, and then go back and call her and let her know what happened. Then I want you to call me. I'll give you my cell phone number and let me know when she will be back at the house. I'll need to talk to her. I'll also want your full names and home addresses," Detective Morrison mentioned to the other two men standing there.

"I'll do that officer. What happens now?" Fred Bellows asked.

"I'm going to call the medical examiner to come out here to review the accident scene and do what he needs to do for his investigation. He will have the body moved to a hospital and prepare it for an autopsy. I'll be back in touch with you if I have more questions. I'll ask you not to go anywhere for the next couple of days. This has all the appearances of an accident so I don't think a full investigation is necessary, but I'm not sure yet."

"What about my golf clubs?" Fred asked.

"Leave every thing like it is. After the coroner is finished we'll clean things up and I'll let you know where you can pick up your things, or depending on the timing I may bring them over to you when I talk to the wife of the deceased." He then got the addresses of the other two golfers and told them they were free to go." He looked at Fred and said, "Do you need a ride anywhere?"

"No," Fred responded. "I'll walk back to the club house and get my car. The walk will do me good."

"Do you have your car keys or are they in the cart?" asked Detective Morrison.

"I didn't think about that," responded Fred. "They are in my golf bag. Do you mind if I go down and get them out?"

"Leave things as they are. I'll ask the paramedics to get the fire engine to drop you off at your rental house."

"No, the house is on the golf course. I can walk from here." Fred said

Fred started walking back through the golf course, following the cart path and watching for oncoming golfers. He started to formulate his next plan but had a hard time getting the sound of the club hitting Tom out of his mind. He had never done anything like this before and felt a little sick over the whole thing. He kept trying to put the experience out of his thoughts and knew he had to concentrate on what he was going to say to Pam when he called her, and how he was going to accomplish the steps he had in his mind.

Fred walked up to the rental house and found the door locked. He remembered where the key was hidden outside and retrieved it and unlocked the door. He then went to the bathroom to relieve himself and as he finished, he dropped to his knees and threw up. He felt terrible as he flushed the toilet, still thinking of the sound of the club hitting Tom and the sound of the snapping of bones in Tom's neck. He washed his face in cold water, looked at himself in the mirror and thought, *You're now a killer, you asshole. Come on, pull yourself together and complete the plan. You can't stop now.*

After standing there a minute, he collected his thoughts and went to the house phone to call Pam. He discovered he had Tom's cell phone number programmed in his cell phone, but nothing for Pam.

Somewhat relieved, he knew then he had to call George Mitchell as that was the only number he had for the three people who were antiquing that morning. He looked at his cell phone as it displayed the number and punched in the numbers on the house phone.

CHAPTER 11

Detective Wilt Morrison watched Fred Bellows as he walked back up the golf cart path leaving to go to his rental house. *He didn't seem too broken up about the death of his friend,* he thought.

He then turned toward the accident scene and stood there carefully looking at the overturned golf cart. He studied the placement of the golf clubs, and how the body landed after being thrown out of the cart. The cart had gone over the side of the hill, turned over completely once and came to rest on its side against some thick brush. Detective Morrison had learned long ago that you needed to look at things to try and find out what was different about a situation, not the way it first looked.

What could be different about this accident that is not the way it looks? That cart had to have been moving pretty good down this hill, Wilt thought. *That being the case, it probably had power to the wheels when it went over the side. If the victim had a heart attack on the way down, his foot probably would have come off the accelerator. If that happened, the retarder on the cart would have stopped or slowed it down. The guy obviously was not trying to commit suicide as that would be a stupid way to do it.*

He looked at the tire marks where the cart went over the hill. He also studied the position of the body relative to where the cart had come to rest. The body was a short way down the hill, quite a ways from the cart. He tried to visualize what would happen if you were riding in the cart and it started to roll over.

You would think that if you were driving the cart and it started to go over the side, you would grab something and try to hang on. If that happened then the body would be closer to where the cart stopped, even if the cart had rolled over his neck and broken it, which is what appeared to have happened. Maybe he was dead before the cart started down the hill. If he were dead, then the body would just fall out as the cart started to tip over. Maybe he got sick or passed out on the way down the hill. Maybe he had a heart attack and died on the way down. In any case, his foot would have come off the accelerator pedal. Once that happened, how could the cart keep accelerating?

Detective Morrison sat down on the side of the hill thinking about all the possibilities.

Was there a fault in the accelerator mechanism? If the cart continued to accelerate by itself, the victim would have jumped out. Would it have continued to run after it turned over? Could something have wedged the accelerator down? Was something caught between the accelerator pedal and the brake pedal?

Detective Morrison continued to try and come up with scenarios that could fit the situation. He could not think of anything plausible except that the cart was under full power when it went over the edge. He concluded that there was no way that could happen unless the accelerator was depressed. He knew that if the driver were incapacitated the cart would stop. Something didn't add up.

He thought of other golf cart accidents that he had heard of while he was on the police force. Either the victim was drunk or the cart had tipped over while the player was on the side of a hill looking for his ball. In this case, the victim knew where his ball was. It was in the sand trap so there was no need to take his eyes off the cart path to look for the ball.

Maybe an animal ran in front of the cart and scared the driver. No, that's too far fetched.

His eyes shifted to the golf clubs, some of which were still in their golf bags, and some were lying outside the bags on the ground.

Are any of those clubs long enough to be wedged between the cart seat and the accelerator?

An idea started to form in his mind. He climbed down the hill and started to look at the victim's golf clubs. Most of the irons were scarred and dirty. The covers on the drivers were cleaner, but still showed some wear. He put on some rubber gloves and pulled an iron out of one of the bags and measured it from the back of the seat to the accelerator. *Not long enough,* he thought to himself. He then looked around and found the longest club, which was the driver that was lying next to some of the clubs that had come out of the bag.

I could make this work. This club could be wedged between the back of the seat and the accelerator.

He looked at the cover and saw some dirt on it. He knew that the forensic lab could see if the dirt on the driver cover and the dirt on the accelerator matched.

Detective Morrison took off the rubber gloves and he walked back up the hill, stood there a few minutes, then walked up the cart path to the tee box. He stood on the area where both of the men had hit their golf balls out in the fairway.

OK, both of them drove their balls out in the fairway. After they each hit their balls, Fred put his driver back in the bag and started walking toward his ball on the right side of the hill, and Tom put his driver in his bag, got in the cart and started down the hill. At least that is what I was told happened.

He remembered what Fred had told him, "After they left the green I drove my ball out on the right side of the hill. Tom put his ball on the tee and hit his drive straight down the fairway but it had a slight hook. It landed in the fairway then rolled into the sand bunker right here." Why did they wait until the two golfers ahead of them cleared the green? They could have hit earlier as there is no way they could have reached the green from the tee box. Did they not want the other two golfers to see what was happening?

Wilt studied the ground around the tee box. He didn't notice anything unusual, no out-of-the-ordinary scuff marks, no blood anywhere. As he started to walk toward where the cart should have been parked, he noticed something that he had missed before. There were two long indentations in the grass leading from the tee box toward the cart.

Looks like something or someone was dragged along here and their shoes left these drag marks. I'll have to check the victim's shoes to see if we can tell if there are marks on the toes or the heels.

He tried to visualize what could have happened there on the tee box. He thought of how Fred would have hit his ball then stepped back and let Tom hit his. Then they would have both walked to the golf cart and put their drivers in the bag. Fred then would have pulled out the three clubs he wanted and start to walk toward his ball. Tom would then have started down the hill on the cart path. In that scenario, no one was dragged across the tee box to the golf cart. *But if they were both walking back to the cart, why the drag marks? The victim's friend was clear across the fairway when the cart ran off the path. Maybe Tom was hit with a golf club, then dragged to the cart, put in the seat and started down the hill when the golf club was wedged between the seat and the accelerator,* Detective Morrison thought. *Maybe that would explain the bruise on the side of the victim's head.*

He continued to stand on the tee box thinking about what could have happened there, and why. He pulled out his camera and took four shots of the drag marks in the grass. He was not sure you could see them very well in a picture.

Maybe I should get another golf cart and see if I can replicate the accident. The cart would have to have been moved up the cart path a little ways so it could start down the hill.

He walked to the point where the cart would have started down the hill. He tried to visualize the cart traveling down the cart path.

If the cart started down from here it probably would have made it to where the accident happened. But, it could have gone off the path in any number of places unless someone was guiding it. No one else was near the cart when it went over the side of the hill. Did the killer start the cart down the hill, then run out on the course so he would be away from the cart when it went over the hill?

He kept trying to imagine how it could have happened. He walked down the path and again stood on the cart path and looked down at the cart.

Shit, maybe it happened like the guy said and was just an accident. Why would someone kill his friend unless there was a strong motive? Maybe he is involved with his wife. Hell I don't know. Maybe I'm making too much out of this.

Detective Morrison's thoughts were interrupted when Doctor Larry Gravits, the Medical Examiner, walked up.

CHAPTER 12

Fred's hands were shaking a little as he held the phone. He took a deep breath and dialed the number. He exhaled as heard the ring on the other end.

George Mitchell, his wife Debbie and Pam Decker had been antiquing for the last three hours. They were investigating the many antique shops available in the area. George and Debbie Mitchell were collectors of many different things, but particularly American brilliant cut glass. Both of them enjoyed looking at the excellent detail in the cutting of the glass done in America between 1880 and 1910. There was no question that it was the finest glass produced in that period, but some believe it also was the second original art that America gave to the world (the first being jazz music). George was looking at a piece cut by the T. G. Hawkes Company of Corning, New York and had to put it down when he felt his phone vibrate.

George picked up his cell phone and looked at the lighted window to see who was calling. As he didn't have the rental house number programmed in his phone, it just indicated an incoming call.

"This is George," he answered.

"George, this is Fred. I have some very bad news, very bad news."

"What is it Fred?"

"There has been a terrible accident. Tom ran off a cliff in the golf cart and was killed."

There was a moment of silence on the phone and then George said, "What?"

"I said Tom was killed when his golf cart ran off a cliff."

"Jesus, are you OK?" George asked.

"I wasn't with him when it happened. I was clear across the fairway looking for my golf ball."

"Damn," George muttered.

"Someone has to inform Pam," Fred went on. "She has to be told. She's with you and Debbie so I guess you are the one who has to break the news."

"I'm in the middle of a goddamn antique store," George responded. "How the hell do I tell her that her husband's been killed in this atmosphere?"

"I'm sure you will think of something," Fred said. "Let me know when you will be coming back here as the detective looking into the accident wants to talk to Tom's wife."

"Why is a detective looking into the situation? I though you said it was an accident?" George asked

"It was, but I guess anytime there is a death you have to get the authorities involved. I was there and saw the whole thing. It was an accident, no question about that."

"OK, I'll see what I can do. I would guess we will be back at the house in probably a half hour to forty-five minutes. It kind of depends on how Pam takes the news. Damn, what a terrible thing to have happened."

"Thanks George, sorry to put this on you but I really had no choice. We can't wait until you three come back to the house. Pam needs to know what happened."

"I know, I know," responded George. "We'll see you later."

The phone connection was broken, and George stood there searching for his wife and Pam. He saw them a couple of aisles over looking at an oak table and talking to each other about it. He looked at Pam and thought what a terrible thing to have happen, just when she was so happy about winning the money so she and Tom could move back to Phoenix. He wandered over closer to the two women and caught his wife's eye and motioned her to join him. Debbie strolled over, leaving Pam looking at some other furniture in the booth with the oak table.

"Fred just called me with some terrible news," George said. "He told me that there was an accident on the golf course. The golf cart Tom was driving tipped over, and Tom was killed."

"My God, George, that's terrible," Debbie whispered.

"I know," George said. "We have to tell Pam. We can't tell her in the middle of an antique store."

"How did it happen?" Debbie asked. "Is Fred all right?"

"Fred was not in the cart when it turned over. We can get the details later. Right now we have to figure a way to let Pam know."

They both stood there looking at each other and thinking of what to do.

"Tell Pam that I'm not feeling well," George added. "We'll act like we're going home and when we get to the car I'll let her know what happened. You can get in the back seat with her and talk to her as we head back to Russell Cove."

"All right," Debbie responded. She walked over to Pam and told her that George was not feeling well, and they probably should go back to the house. Pam looked a little puzzled but started to walk out of the store, following Debbie and George.

"I'm sorry you are not feeling well," Pam said.

George didn't say anything but continued to walk to the car. When they reached the car he turned to Pam and said, "Pam, there has been a terrible accident."

"What?" She responded looking at George.

"Fred called me a few minutes ago. He told me that on the golf course this morning Tom was driving the cart, and it went over a cliff. The cart rolled on top of him, and he was killed. I'm sorry but there is no other way to tell you."

Pam looked at George with a pained look and said, "What do you mean? What are you talking about? You must be mistaken."

"No, I'm not mistaken. I'm really sorry to tell you this, but that's what happened. I think we should go back to the house."

"I can't believe this. My God, how could something like this happen? Tom is dead? No, it's not possible. Tom is dead? I can't believe it. Tom is dead?" She started to lean against the car and kept saying she could not believe it. She then looked at Debbie and leaned against her and started to cry. "Tom is dead? No, it's not possible. We just moved to Reno, and were planning to return to Phoenix. Tom is gone? Oh God, how did this happen, how did this happen?"

Debbie put her arms around her and held her and said, "I'm so sorry Pam. I'm so sorry."

Pam kept crying and her body went limp as she leaned against Debbie. "What am I going to do without Tom?" she moaned. "What am I going to do?"

"Let's get in the car and go back to the house," Debbie whispered "Come on now, everyone will be there to help you through this."

George opened the car door, and Debbie helped Pam into the back seat. She got in beside her, and Pam put her head on Debbie's shoulder and kept crying. George started the car and pulled out in the street and headed for Russell Cove. George wondered what really happened out there on the golf course. He felt a little sick as he looked in the rear view mirror and saw Pam's body shaking with sobs as she leaned against Debbie.

Damn, he thought, *this is going to be a rough next couple of days.*

CHAPTER 13

Fred Bellows hung up the phone after talking to George. He then took out the card that Detective Wilt Morrison gave him and called the cell number. He told Detective Morrison that Tom's wife would be back at the house in about a half hour. He could talk to her then, if she was up to it. He asked the detective when he could get his golf clubs back and was surprised at the response.

"We're going to hold on to the golf clubs for a couple of days," Detective Morrison said.

"Why is that?" Fred asked.

"Just routine," Detective Morrison responded. "I'll bring your car keys to you when I stop by the house, but the clubs will stay with us for a couple of days."

"But what if I want to play golf again just to get my mind off this accident?" Fred asked.

"Well, you'll have to rent some," Detective Morrison responded rather curtly.

"OK, then we'll see you in an hour or so," Fred said. He said goodbye and hung up. He was not comfortable about the detective keeping his golf clubs.

Did I wipe my driver clean after I hit Tom? He thought. *Can they find pieces of hair on the clubs? Damn, I wish I could remember what I did with that driver. Maybe when I put it back in the head cover the inside of the cover wiped it clean.*

Fred put the club problem out of his mind and started looking for the turkey baster that he had seen in the kitchen drawer the night before while looking for a wine opener.

I have no idea why they have something to baste a turkey with in the drawer. Maybe one of the groups had a Thanksgiving dinner up here. It's a good thing it's here as I can use it, he thought.

Fred Bellows took the turkey baster and went out in the garage. He looked through the garbage from the dinner the night before and found an empty wine bottle. He picked up the bottle and went to Tom's car and found it unlocked as he suspected. He pulled the hood latch, located the brake fluid reservoir and pulled off the cap. He remembered that a few years ago he was talking to a mechanic and was told his car needed brake fluid. He told the mechanic to go ahead and add the fluid and watched him empty the brake fluid reservoir. The mechanic used a wet vacuum to get the fluid out of the engine. The mechanic told Fred that if he wanted to change the fluid at home, that a turkey baster was a good tool to use to extract the fluid. Fred always remembered that conversation and every time he saw a turkey baster he thought of brake fluid.

Fred took the turkey baster and started sucking out the brake fluid and putting it in the wine bottle. He had to estimate how much fluid he took out as he wanted some brake fluid left in the braking system. When he thought he had enough fluid to affect the braking action on the car, he then grabbed a shovel and went to the back yard. He dug a hole and put the wine bottle full of braking fluid in the hole and covered it up.

He went back to the car, pulled out the instruction manual from the glove box and started flipping through the pages. He studied the section on "fuses" and when he learned what he needed, he located the fuse box in the car and pulled out the Brake Warning Light fuse and the Anti-Lock Brake Warning Light fuse and put the fuse box back in its place.

She's going to be too distraught to notice that the warning lights don't flash when she turns on the ignition, he thought. *If I planned this right, the brakes will have enough fluid in them and continue to work until she gets some miles down the road then what little fluid is left will probably overheat and she will lose her brakes.*

He took the two fuses out to the yard with the shovel and dug another hole. He put the fuses in the hole and covered them up.

I have to talk her into driving the car back home, he thought. *I have to figure that if she has an accident and the car is all smashed up they probably will not discover that the fuses are gone. It will be put in the books as an accident of an upset widow who was driving too fast. That will be one less couple to collect the lottery money.*

Fred took the turkey baster back in the kitchen, washed it out with soap and put it back in the kitchen drawer. After thinking about it for a few moments, he thought he should probably call his wife Ginger and let her know what had happened.

Ginger was wine tasting with the two other couples, Jim and Linda Schroeder and Dave and Norma Wheeler. She could relay the message to all of them if they were together. Fred was sure they would all return to the house as soon as they found out the news. He called Ginger, told her about the accident. She could not believe it and started to ask a lot of questions about how it happened. Fred tried to tell her what happened and how the cart overturned, but she kept interrupting him with more questions. He finally told her that details could be gone over once they came back to the house. Fred could tell that Ginger was upset. She wanted to ask more questions, but hesitated knowing Fred would not say much more. Ginger said she would let the others know and they all would probably return to the house to support Pam.

Fred thought about what Ginger has said. They were going to come back to the house and "support Pam." Once again he felt his heart rate start to go up. He thought of Pam, and how he enjoyed being around her.

What if she notices something wrong as soon as she tries to stop the car? That could be just down the street. What if her brakes hold until she gets to where she is going? What if someone else goes with her and can tell something is wrong with the brakes?

He thought about going out, digging up the bottle and putting the brake fluid back in the car. He sat down in the living room and tried to calm himself.

I was the only one here alone and someone will figure out it was me that screwed with the car if she doesn't get very far. OK, Fred, calm down. You have already killed her husband, and that went well. Now you have to get rid of Pam, as doing away with only one half of a couple will not do any good.

He felt himself getting calmer as he pondered the possibilities. He was sure his plan would work as long as no one else went with Pam.

What if someone else does go with Pam? As long as it's not my wife Ginger, that would be OK. In fact it may be better if someone else went along. For each couple that cannot claim the money means more for Ginger and me.

He put his head back on the couch and closed his eyes. He could not get rid of the image of Tom's body in his lap.

I wish to hell I never invested in that land deal. I would not be in this mess except for my damn greed. Four million dollars would have been just fine. Well, if everything goes according to plan, we'll still be all right.

He tried to relax, knowing that guilt feelings will surge through his body when he sees Pam.

CHAPTER 14

Detective Wilt Morrison, while chewing on his cigar, explained to the Medical Examiner what had happened, or at least what he was told had happened.

"Well, let's go down and look at the scene," said Larry Gravits after the initial discussion with Detective Morrison.

"It just seems strange to me how a golf cart can turn over and break someone's neck," mused Detective Morrison as he was chewing on his cigar while they were walking toward the accident area.

"It certainly is possible," relayed Larry. "The cart can roll over on a person and break his neck, or throw him out and the person lands on his head. It has happened before, although I agree with you it is rather rare."

As they approached the scene where the accident happened, Larry put on his rubber gloves and stood there looking over the area. He then walked down to where the body was lying and bent down and examined the area where the neck was broken. He took out his camera and took several pictures of the body. He then moved the dead man's neck back and forth taking further notice of the face and head.

"This is rather strange," he mentioned as he rotated the head. "It looks like a twist fracture, and there is no indentation where the cart could have rolled over on his neck. If his neck was broken due to the accident, there should be an indication that he landed on top of his head and caught part of his body in the cart as it rolled over. There does not seem to be any excess dirt on top of his hat where the twisting motion could have occurred. I see some bruising on the side of the head, perhaps where the cart could have hit him."

"What about the location of the body relative to where the cart landed?" asked Detective Morrison.

"It appears that he rolled out of the cart just as it was turning over," responded Larry. "That is also unusual as you would think that he would have either tried to get out or grabbed something to hang onto as he went off the side of the hill."

"My cell phone is ringing," said Detective Morrison as he walked a few feet away and answered his phone.

Larry continued to study the area and looked at the golf clubs, some of which were still in the bags and some were thrown on the side of the hill. In a few minutes Detective Morrison returned and said, "That was the guy that was riding with the victim. He told me that the wife will be back at the house in a half hour or so. He seems a little concerned when I told him that we will not return his golf clubs for a couple of days. I think we should look at the clubs to see if there is anything on them besides dirt and grass."

"What are you thinking?" asked Larry

"Well, I'm not sure yet, but it seems to me that maybe the guy was already dead before the cart went off the side of the hill."

"How did the cart get down the hill?" asked Larry.

"You could wedge the golf club called the driver between the seat and the accelerator, and the cart would go until it hit something or ran off down the hill."

"But the golf drivers are both covered and in the bags," responded Larry

"That could have been done before we arrived here. The victim's partner could have cleaned up the area even before the two witnesses arrived."

Larry then went over and took a close look at the drivers in the bags. "Who was driving the cart? Do you know which bag was the victim's?" he asked.

"Look at the name tags on the bags."

Larry went down to the overturned cart and looked at the golf bags. "The one on the driver's side has the name of Fred Bellows. The one on the passenger's side says Tom Decker. Which one is the victim?"

"Tom Decker is the victim. That means the clubs on the driver's side belong to his partner, Fred Bellows. Take a look at his driver and see what you can get from it."

LAST WALK AT RUSSELL COVE

Larry took a close look at the head cover of Fred's driver. "Nothing unusual here," he said. He then took a picture of the head cover while it was on the club and slowly removed the cover and studied the club face.

"I don't see anything on the club face. But maybe we can detect something from a closer examination. In fact we can look at all the clubs to determine if there is any residual hair or skin tissue." He then examined Tom's driver cover.

"There are some smudges on the top of this head cover," he said. "I should take some pictures of this head cover as maybe some of the smudges will match the metallic markings on the accelerator. So you think maybe the victim was hit with a golf club before the accident? If that's the case how did he get his neck broken?"

"His partner could have hit him with a club, twisted his limp neck and broken it, then dragged him to the cart. He then could have wedged the driver down on the accelerator and let the cart run down the hill until it ran off the cliff," said Detective Morrison surprising himself somewhat as those thoughts popped into his mind.

That would explain the two drag marks I saw on the tee box, he thought.

"Check the back of the victim's shoes. See if there are any grass stains on the back of his heels."

Larry went over to the body and looked at the back of the shoes. "There are some grass stains here," he said. "Those could come from walking around on the golf course. They don't look too suspicious but we can't tell for sure yet." He snapped some more pictures.

"We really will not be sure about the neck break until I do the autopsy. That will tell us a lot about how the neck was broken, but I'd bet my bottom dollar that it will show a strong, quick twist did it. I know it may be possible that it happened when the cart turned over, but I don't think so."

Larry Gravits looked around and then said, "I think we're about finished here. Let's let the paramedics take the body to the hospital. We'll collect the golf clubs, and I'll put them in my car and have them looked at as soon as I can get them to a lab."

Detective Morrison helped Larry gather the materials that were spread on the side of the hill. They were very careful not to let anything touch that was not already against something else. He walked up and put the two golf balls that were still on the fairway in plastic bags and included them in the materials to be held. When things were cleaned up, he called the clubhouse, explained to them what had happened (which somehow they already knew) and told them to come out and pick up the golf cart. He instructed the club manager to have the cart stored separately and not disturbed in case they wanted to examine it further. He looked at his watch and decided it was time to go visit the wife of the victim.

CHAPTER 15

After Ginger Bellows finished the call from her husband, she flipped her phone closed and thought of what she was going to say to the wine tasting group. They were all lined up at a tasting bar in a new little winery that Jim Schroeder wanted to visit. The rest of the group wanted to go to a well-known winery, but Jim insisted they stop here first.

That morning before they left the house, Jim was looking in his medical bag for some aspirin and came across the cyanide that he had purchased for the neighbor's dog. He looked at the pills and started thinking about the lottery money and the blackmail.

How can I use these cyanide pills on our wine tasting sojourn? he thought to himself.

He needed more money than the lottery ticket was going to give him to protect himself from the potential law suits.

With a couple more million I can buy off the nurses, he thought.

As he stood there, a plan started to form in his mind. He thought that if they visited a new winery it could be a place where a couple of people could die from cyanide poisoning. It would have to be a new winery because most new, small wineries do not grow their own grapes but purchase them from several different vineyards. If he watched carefully, he could slip a couple of pills in someone's wine glass. The wine would have to come from a newly opened bottle and that particular wine could only be poured into the two glasses where he slipped the cyanide pills. As the two victims were dying, everyone would be distracted and he could put a cyanide pill in the newly opened bottle. This way it would look like the cyanide came in the bottle and had poisoned the only two people who drank from that bottle. There would be an investigation and a long period of research to determine where that particular wine came from and how the cyanide got into the wine. The focus around the two deaths would be toward the winery, not toward Jim Schroeder.

The first small winery that they visited was not very crowded. Jim watched carefully as Dave and Norma selected the wines they wanted to taste. He studied the bottles that were being used. The first few rounds of tasting, the bottles that were already opened were used. When a new bottle was uncorked, he watched as more than two glasses were poured from it. At the first winery the proper situation never developed. He had to continue to watch and wait.

Although the group wanted to stop at a well known winery, Jim Schroeder kept insisting that they visit a couple more new wineries. He wanted to make sure they stayed on the track of wineries that did not grow their own grapes.

The second winery was also relatively new and small. Things were getting a little more crowded now, and there were several people lined up at the tasting bar tasting wine. Once again Jim watched closely as bottles were opened, and wine was poured. He noticed that Dave and Norma Wheeler were asking for a specific Merlot that was on the tasting list. The wine seller did not see any bottle open and reached under the tasting bar to get a new bottle. Jim reached in his pocket and started to finger the three cyanide pills he had brought. The wine salesman poured the newly opened wine in the glasses of Dave and Norma. Ginger Bellows walked away from the bar as she had a phone call. Jim watched where the wine salesman placed the newly opened bottle and started moving slowly toward Dave and Norma. He stood there for a moment waiting for the proper moment to drop the pills.

"Can I talk to each of you please?" Ginger Bellows asked. "I just received a call from Fred and he has some bad news that you need to hear. Would you mind stepping away from the tasting area and come toward me?"

Jim Schroeder watched as Dave and Norma Wheeler left their wine and walked toward Ginger. He knew he had lost the moment, and started walking with them.

Maybe I can get this done at the next wine tasting, or when we come back in, he thought.

As they gathered around Ginger Bellows, she told them about

Tom's accident and received various reactions, mostly all shock and sorrow.

"I think we should return to Russell Cove and be there for Pam," Ginger said.

They all agreed and started to head back to their cars. They had taken two cars as Dave and Norma Wheeler were not sure if they were going to stay with Jim and Linda Schroeder all the time so they had driven their own car. As the two couples and Fred's wife Ginger got in the cars to return home, Jim Schroeder swore under his breath that Tom's death had screwed up his own plans.

CHAPTER 16

When George, Debbie and Pam returned from antiquing and walked into the rental house, Fred Bellows was sitting downstairs in the living room. He immediately got up to greet his friends. He noticed that Pam's eyes were red, and she was unsteady on her feet. He walked to her and wrapped his arms around her.

"I'm so sorry Pam," Fred said.

He continued to hug her until she finally broke away. They walked into the living room and sat down.

"Once again, I can't tell you how sorry I am Pam," Fred stated. "It was a crazy accident. I don't really know how it happened."

"Tell me what happened," she said

Fred went through the scenario, as he had for the fourth time and when he finished Pam just sat there and looked at him.

"I still cannot believe it," she said "I just can't believe it. Where is Tom's body now?"

"They are going to take him to the hospital for an autopsy," Fred stated. "I guess that's routine in any accident where someone dies."

"Who do I talk to about where he is and when the autopsy will be finished?" Pam asked.

"There is a detective named Morrison who came to the accident scene. He said he will come by here when he is finished his investigation as he wants to talk to you about Tom," Fred added.

"What does he want to talk about? I thought it was an accident."

"I'm not sure what he wants," Fred responded. "He was asking me questions about Tom's health because maybe he had a heart attack when he was going down the cart path."

"He didn't have a heart condition. As far as I know he didn't have any health problems," Pam said.

"I didn't say anything to the detective about the lottery ticket. I thought it best to keep it quiet so it will not complicate things," Fred mentioned.

"How would it complicate things?" Pam asked.

"I'm not really sure, but there is no real reason anyone has to know about it," Fred responded

"While we were coming back to the house," George Mitchell said as he tried to quickly change the subject, "Pam has decided to call her son in Phoenix and see if he can fly down and be with her."

"I need someone to help me through this, and there are a lot of flights from Phoenix to San Francisco. I'm sure he can get a flight this afternoon and make it to The City by late afternoon or early evening."

"That's a good idea," Fred Bellows agreed. "Perhaps you could drive down to the airport in San Francisco and pick him up when he arrives. In fact it probably would be a good idea to perhaps stay the night by the airport where you two could have dinner and decide a few things before coming back to the house."

"I like that idea, Fred. After we find out when he's coming in, I'll call for a hotel by the airport." Pam looked in her purse, pulled out her address book and asked George if he would make the call to her son Taylor. She asked him to explain to him what had happened and ask him if he could get a flight to San Francisco this afternoon so he could be with her. George agreed, took the number, and walked up to the kitchen to use the phone. He tried to organize his thoughts as he knew he would have to explain to Taylor that his father had been killed, and his mother needs him.

"God, I have to think of all the things I have to do now," Pam said sadly.

As George was dialing the phone, the doorbell rang.

"I'll get it," said Fred Bellows. "It's probably the detective." Fred really did not feel comfortable seeing Detective Morrison, but he took a deep breath, tried to put a look of confidence on his face, and went to the door.

It has to be determined an accident, he thought. *There is no reason that it can be called anything else, so relax and be yourself.* He went to the door and opened it.

CHAPTER 17

Detective Wilt Morrison thought about the situation as he started to go and visit with Tom Decker's wife. He was convinced that there had been foul play in the rollover of the golf cart and believed the autopsy would prove him right. He didn't have enough to charge Fred Bellows with any crime yet, but he thought he could make him sweat a little. He anticipated Fred to be at the house when he talked to Pam Decker and began thinking of the questions he was going ask Pam and also the questions that he was going to ask Fred.

I wonder if I can get the guy to slip up with his story, Wilt thought. *I'll have him tell me one more time and ask some questions as he goes through it to let him think I'm suspicious of him.*

He found the house, put his cigar in the car's ashtray, and rang the doorbell. After a couple of minutes the door opened. Detective Morrison saw Fred Bellows standing there.

"Good afternoon detective," Fred said as he swung the door open.

Detective Morrison looked at him and didn't say anything. He just stood there and stared at Fred.

"Come on in and I'll introduce you to Pam Decker," Fred relayed and started to walk back into the house.

"Don't go anywhere Mr. Bellows as I would like to talk to you after I'm finished with Mrs. Decker," Detective Morrison said rather forcefully.

"Sure, no problem."

As they walked down to the living room, Detective Morrison noticed two women sitting on the sofa and a man talking in low tones on the phone. One woman had blood shot eyes, and he guessed that was the widow.

"Pam, this is Detective Morrison, the detective I was telling you about who wanted to talk to you," Fred said, pointing to Wilt.

"Mrs. Decker, I'm very sorry about your loss. I know this is a bad time, but do you mind answering a few questions for me?" Detective Morrison asked.

"No, no. It's quite all right. I'll do what I can," Pam replied.

Detective Morrison turned to Fred and the other woman sitting on the couch and asked them if they minded that he spoke to Mrs. Decker alone. Fred and Debbie got up to leave when George came into the room.

"I'm George Mitchell," he said to the detective, "and this is my wife Debbie." He then turned to Pam and told her that her son Taylor was handling the news OK and would arrive in San Francisco this evening at 6:45 pm on a United flight.

"I'll give you all the details later," he said to Pam. He then joined Fred and Debbie and walked out of the room.

Detective Morrison waited about a minute to make sure everyone was out of hearing range then started to talk to Pam.

"I understand that the cart tipped over and rolled on him, and he died from a broken neck. Is that what happened?" she asked trying not to start crying again.

"That's what appears to have happened. Did your husband have life insurance?" he asked.

"Yes, I think it is around four or five hundred thousand, plus what he may get from a death benefit from his company. Why do you ask?"

"Well, one of the reasons I'm asking you these questions is that the insurance company is going to be very curious about what happened, and I need to have all the answers. Did your husband have any type of heart problems or any other health issues?"

"No. He had prostate cancer about five years ago. He had it removed and nothing has shown up since then."

"How about any changes in his life, like any financial problems?"

Pam hesitated and thought about the gambling losses, and then the lottery ticket. She was not sure what to say. *I best be safe,* she thought. "No, not that I can think of," she answered.

"Why did you hesitate to answer me?" Detective Morrison said.

"Well, we moved to Reno about a year ago, and Tom has a new job. We have spent some money fixing up the house. I didn't know if that was what you wanted to know. It wasn't really a financial hardship."

"Has your husband been depressed lately or have you noticed any change in his attitude or his demeanor?"

"What's all this have to do with the accident? You're making it sound like he may have committed suicide."

"We find it a little strange that a healthy, happy man would let a golf cart run off a cliff."

"Tom would never take his own life. He had a lot to live for. In fact we had decided to move back to Phoenix. We were both looking forward to that. Perhaps there was a malfunction with the golf cart."

"The cart has been quarantined," Detective Morrison said. "We have a mechanic going over it as we speak."

"When will you be finished with Tom's body?" she asked, feeling her eyes starting to tear up again.

"Once again, I'm sorry for you loss, Mrs. Decker. The autopsy should be finished tomorrow afternoon. I will notify you when it's done. You can make arrangements to have your husband's remains sent to the mortuary of your choice."

The front door opened and five people came in and walked down to the living room where Detective Morrison was sitting with Pam.

"Oh Pam," Ginger Bellows said. "What happened?"

After a few minutes of consoling Pam, the five individuals looked at Detective Morrison and introduced themselves.

Detective Morrison asked them their names again as he wrote each name down in his note pad. It was Dave and Norma Wheeler, Dr. Jim and Linda Schroeder and Ginger Bellows.

"I'm just getting ready to leave," Detective Morrison said. "I need to spend a moment with Fred Bellows before I go. Would someone find him and ask him to come back to the living room?"

Dave Wheeler went and found Fred and asked him to come back into the living room. George and Debbie Mitchell also returned and asked if it was all right that they were there too.

Detective Morrison nodded his head in approval. He then looked at Jim Schroeder and asked, "Did you say you were a doctor?"

"Yes I am," Jim answered.

"It seems that the cart rolled over on Mr. Decker, and it appears that he broke his neck in a twisting motion. Does that seem plausible doctor?" Detective Morrison asked as he looked at Fred.

"I don't know, I'm a heart surgeon," replied Jim. "I guess it could have happened that way. I'm sure stranger things have happened."

Detective Morrison stood there for a moment, and then said to Fred Bellows, "Did you handle Mr. Decker's golf clubs while you were playing today?"

Fred looked a little nervous and replied, "I don't know. I guess there were times when I picked up his clubs from the green when we were finished putting. Why do you ask?"

"What about his driver? Did you handle that?" Detective Morrison asked ignoring Fred's question.

Fred thought a moment, remembering he handled Tom's driver with his gloved hand. "No I don't think I did." *Did I touch the driver with my right hand when I put it back in his bag?* he wondered.

"About how much time was there between the time you started walking toward your ball and Mr. Decker started the cart down the hill?" Detective Morrison asked.

"Well, it could not have been more than a couple of minutes. I walked over to the cart and put in my driver and pulled out the other clubs. Tom was putting his club in his bag as I started walking. It could not have been more than a couple of minutes. Why are you asking?"

"Just wondering," said Detective Morrison. "What about his golf balls, did you handle any of those?"

Shit, are my finger prints on the ball I tossed into the sand bunker? "I recall passing golf balls back and forth and talking about the markings we make on the balls to identify which ball is ours," he said.

"If I recall, Mr. Decker hit his ball first before you hit yours. Is that correct?" Detective Morrison asked Fred.

"No, I hit my ball first," Fred responded. *What the hell is he trying to do, get me to change my story?* he thought.

Detective Morrison looked at his notebook. "Yes, that's right. That's what you told me. Why did you wait until the two golfers in front of you were off the green before you hit your ball?"

"No particular reason, I guess. It's just nicer to play on a course where you think you are the only ones playing," Fred said. *Why is he asking me that?*

Detective Morrison turned to Pam Decker and said, "Once again let me say how sorry I am for your loss." He then turned to Fred Bellows and said, "I'll be in touch." He then walked to the door and closed it as he left.

Detective Morrison got in his car, put the cigar back in his mouth and started the car.

I still think that Fred Bellows has something to hide, he thought as he started the car and drove away.

"What was that all about?" Dave Wheeler asked Fred as they were all standing there after Detective Morrison left.

"What was what all about?" Fred responded rather defensively.

"Well, the detective seemed to question you rather pointedly, don't you think? I wonder why he was doing that?" George Mitchell said.

"Damned if I know. I guess he is trying to cover all the basis so he can safely say it was an accident. As I said before, I didn't see the accident as I was clear across the fairway. I have two witnesses that saw me running toward the accident after it happened. I feel as bad about this as everyone else."

CHAPTER 18

The four couples plus Pam Decker sat around the living room discussing the situation and what Pam was going to do now. She was reminded that Taylor, her son, was arriving at the San Francisco airport at 6:45 this evening. The discussion then centered on the fact if Pam was in any condition to drive to San Francisco by herself to be with her son.

"It's only about an hour's drive," Pam said. "I'm sure I can handle it. I think it would be best if Taylor and I get a hotel room, had dinner and came up here tomorrow. That way we can get things settled, and he can help me think things through."

"No way are you driving down there by yourself," Ginger Bellows cut in.

"I'm sure she will be OK," Fred Bellows said rather quickly. "Besides how will you get back if you ride down with her?"

"You could follow us down and bring me back," Ginger responded.

Fred had to think of something to keep his wife from going to San Francisco with Pam. "I'm sure she will be OK honey," he responded. "This whole thing has me upset too as I was there. I'd like you to be with me at this time."

Ginger looked at her husband rather strangely and wondered why all of a sudden he needed her.

"Fred's right," Pam said. "I can go alone. It's only about an hour, and I'll be just fine."

"I know this is a bad time, but when are we going to discuss what we are going to do with the lottery ticket?" asked George Mitchell.

"Yes it is a bad time," said Debbie, his wife. "George can't you see that there are more important things to discuss right now?"

"We'll get to it all in good time," Jim Schroeder added. "Pam," he said as he walked over close to her, "If you want, I can give you something to make you sleep well tonight."

"I don't think so. After a nice dinner with Taylor, I'm sure I'll feel better, and it will be OK."

"I hate to bring this up," Dave Wheeler said, "but you better think about leaving if you want to get to San Francisco by 6:30 or so. The traffic can get real thick in the city in the afternoon."

"I'll put some things in my suitcase and take them with me." She started to get up from the couch to walk to her bedroom, and then hesitated, thinking about going in the room with all of Tom's things still lying around.

"Why don't you sit down a minute?" said Norma Wheeler. "Let me go into the room and straighten it up a little." She then proceeded to disappear into Tom and Pam's room. After a few minutes she returned. She told Pam she thought it would be better now if she entered.

"Do you have an extra set of car keys?" asked Fred. "I think Tom's keys are still in his golf bag with the authorities."

"Yes, I have an extra set in my purse."

As Pam went into her room to get enough things for her overnight in San Francisco, the rest of the group sat around and were staring at nothing, all lost in their own thoughts.

"What a terrible thing to happen," Norma Wheeler said.

"Just when Tom and Pam were going to be happy with their winnings and move back to Phoenix," Debbie Mitchell added.

"What are we having for dinner?" asked George.

"George," his wife Debbie responded, "You always bring up the wrong things at the wrong time."

"Well, we're going to have to eat sometime. Is someone cooking dinner here tonight?"

"I'm not hungry," said Fred Bellows. "What I would like to do is just have a snack and sit in the Jacuzzi for about an hour. Ginger, are you up for that?"

"I'd like that," responded his wife Ginger. "Sitting there with a glass of wine and relaxing sounds good to me."

"I'll need something more than that," added George. "I'd like to take Debbie out to an early dinner. This way nobody has to cook so it will be easier."

"That sounds good to me," Jim Schroeder mentioned as he thought of the cyanide pills he still had in his pocket. "What about it Linda?"

"OK, just let me put up my feet for awhile, and I'll be ready to go."

"I think Dave and I will join you," Norma Wheeler said. "Is that all right with you Dave?"

"Sure. That's fine with me," Dave responded.

Pam came out of her bedroom with a small traveling bag in her hand.

"Are you sure you will be all right?" Debbie Mitchell asked once again.

"Yes, I'm OK. I just need to pick up Taylor so we can get some planning done."

"Do you have our phone numbers in your phone in case you need to call us?" asked George Mitchell.

"I think so, but let me check," Pam said as she reached for her cell phone. "I have both Debbie and Ginger in here so that should be fine."

"Who do you have under ICE?" asked Fred Bellows.

"What's ICE?" asked Pam.

"That stands for In Case of an Emergency," Fred said. "It's a number that paramedics use if an individual is unconscious for some reason. You probably should put Taylor's number under that description when you have time."

"Right now I don't have the time or the patience to change my phone," Pam responded.

"Here let me do it," George told her. "What's Taylor's number?"

"I don't have his cell phone. He changed his number a week ago. I only have his home phone. Tom has Taylor's cell phone in his phone. Where is Tom's phone?"

"It's probably with his golf bag. The detective still has all that until tomorrow," Fred Bellows volunteered.

"Look," George Mitchell explained, "I'll put in my cell number, and then you can change it tonight or tomorrow when Taylor gets in."

"Fine," Pam responded looking a little impatient. She handed him the phone and waited while George entered the number then handed her back her phone. Pam took the phone and headed for the front door.

They all walked to the car and hugged Pam before she got in. Fred Bellows seemed to hug her a little longer than necessary. They watched as Pam started the car and backed out of the driveway. She gave them a slight wave as she started down the hill toward Highway 1. They stood there as the car disappeared in the distance.

It's a real shame I have to do this. But so far, so good, Fred Bellows thought. *She didn't notice that the warning lights didn't come on, as I suspected. Now somewhere down the road I hope I took enough fluid out so the brakes will eventually fail.*

CHAPTER 19

Pam thought she would go through Sebastopol as she believed it was the quickest way to the freeway. She was also familiar with the route. She noticed as she stopped at a stop sign leading onto the highway that she had to push rather hard on the brakes for the car to come to a complete stop. She made a mental note to talk to Taylor about the brakes on the car and maybe have them looked at. She also felt a little guilty when she started to get upset with her late husband Tom for not taking care of the brakes.

Her thoughts turned to the tasks and problems that lay ahead. She still had a hard time believing that her husband was dead. She thought of the good times they had together since their marriage, and she thought of the bad times she had since they moved to Reno. She kept getting waves of guilt feelings when she thought about Sheldon Monroe.

She carefully drove into Sebastopol and had to pump the brakes to stop the car at a stoplight. She turned on to Highway 12 and started toward the 101 freeway. As she drove her thoughts went back to the situation she was in.

Her emotions were swinging back and forth from feeling sorry for herself, to being upset with her husband, to thinking about her future. She felt herself getting frustrated about the situation and all the things she had to do. She thought about her financial situation. She calculated her assets in her mind and started adding the various parts of her financial situation.

Three hundred and fifty thousand dollars in the stock market, she thought. *Add that to the million dollars in the lottery and the half million that I get for Tom's death insurance, that's not bad. Then maybe I can clear a few thousand when I sell the house. I can probably go back to Phoenix with close to two million dollars, which will put me in good financial shape.*

She started to relax a little as she thought about all the money she was going to have. The road sign came up for 101 South and she pulled onto the freeway heading for San Francisco.

Her mind again began to wander, and as she thought of various things, she started to feel better.

I'm still a young person and not bad looking. With all that money I would be a good catch for some guy looking for female company. Maybe I should go back and talk to Sheldon Monroe, the bartender that likes me. I can't be in too much of a hurry to get out of Reno as now I can gamble for a few weeks or months and not worry about losing money. Maybe I can add to my assets.

Her thoughts then went back to being lonely and by herself, and she got tears in her eyes as she thought of being alone in the big house in Reno. She knew she was going to miss Tom as they had been together for a long time.

Her thoughts went to her son Taylor and how he was going to react about his father's death.

He'll be a big help, she thought. *He'll know what to do and who to contact about funeral arrangements. Should I have Tom buried in Reno or Phoenix? No, Phoenix should be the place. He doesn't have any friends in Reno. I think the only people that know him are in the office where he works. Should he be buried or cremated? We never discussed these things as we thought we would live so much longer. Cremated would probably be better, then I can have a small memorial in Reno and another one in Phoenix and not have to rush into things. A memorial in Phoenix could be in a few weeks. I hope Taylor agrees with me on having him cremated. God, I can't believe I'm even thinking about having my husband cremated. I can't believe he's dead. What about our little granddaughter. She's going to have to grow up hardly knowing here grandfather. What a terrible, terrible thing.*

She was jerked out of her thoughts as she came upon a slow moving car in front of her. She pumped the brakes enough to slow down, looked to her left and moved to the fast lane.

Her thoughts then turned to the detective that talked to her about Tom's accident. She wondered why he was so inquisitive about Tom's state of mind and why he questioned how a healthy, happy man could run his golf cart off the cart path.

If it was a mechanical problem I'll sue the golf course, she thought. *If it wasn't a mechanical problem, what could it have been? He was healthy and ran the cart off the cart path down an embankment. How could that have happened? Was Fred involved as the detective hinted? If so, why? Did it have something to do with winning the lottery? Maybe I should have told the detective about the lottery ticket. Fred didn't want me to say anything about that. I wonder why?*

As she continued to think about Fred's comments and the detective's questions, she felt herself becoming upset. She didn't notice that she had increased her speed because she was lost in thoughts about the possibility of murder.

If it did have something to do with the lottery money, what reason would Fred have to be involved with Tom's accident? We have all been friends for so long. No, Fred would not do a thing like that. But the detective was questioning if the rollover could have killed Tom. The detective was also questioning things like if Fred had touched Tom's golf clubs or his golf ball. I wonder why? I'll talk to Taylor about all this. He can give me some advice on what to do. He will probably want to talk to Fred also. I better talk to Fred directly about all of this when we get back to the house, she thought.

She was approaching the tunnel leading to the Golden Gate Bridge.

She came upon a slow moving landscaping pickup too fast. She realized that she needed to slow down quickly and hit her brakes. The pedal went clear to the floor, and the car slowed very little. She could tell that the car was continuing to move closer to the pickup in front of her. To avoid hitting the pickup she swerved to the left, into the fast lane. Her swerve was too severe, and she sideswiped the center guardrail that separated the north and south lanes.

Damn, I have to get away from this guardrail, she thought. The thought of the damage the rail caused to the car and for a fleeting moment she worried about what Tom would say. Then she remembered he was dead.

Once again she over-corrected, and the car skidded back into traffic, across two southbound lanes into the slow lane and started to roll over. As she moved into the slow lane a large truck smashed into her car. The last thing Pam saw was the freeway coming up at her from the driver's window as the truck forced her car underneath its front axle.

CHAPTER 20

The four couples that stayed at the house while Pam went to meet her son decided to take a short rest before dinner. They retreated to their respective bedrooms to either try to nap or read a book. George and Debbie Mitchell were both trying to relax and read a little, but both were having a hard time concentrating on their reading material. George was concerned about what was going on with their friends and turned to his wife who was lying beside him on the bed.

"Don't you notice anything strange about how everyone is acting?" he said.

"Not particularly. Everyone is really upset about what happened to Tom."

"The first thing is, I don't understand why everyone wants to keep this lottery ticket a secret. What's the big deal about people knowing we've won some money? They're going to find out soon enough. It's like they want to keep all this stuff to themselves."

"I don't think that is so unusual," Debbie responded. "You know once the word gets out, there will be a lot of people contacting us and wanting donations, loans, and so forth. We really need to decide when we are going to split the money."

"If things keep going like they are we will have less people to…" George became silent and thought a moment.

"What?" Debbie asked.

"Didn't you think it was rather strange how Fred acted about Tom's accident? He didn't seem very upset. Then I thought it was unusual how the detective kept looking at Fred and asking questions about touching clubs and things. I also don't really understand why they confiscated Tom's and Fred's golf clubs. It's like they suspect something, and think Fred has something to do with Tom's death."

"Do you really think so? Why would Fred harm Tom?"

"I don't know but remember when we were cooking dinner last night, I heard Jim ask Fred if he was still playing in the real estate market. Ginger said very quickly that she wished he wasn't, then looked as if she had made a mistake. I wonder if Fred and Ginger are in some kind of financial trouble."

"Well, that doesn't mean Fred wants to kill everyone for the lottery money," Debbie said.

"Jesus, Debbie, I hope not," George responded.

George Mitchell lay there in the bed thinking about events and things from the day before and this morning. He thought it was peculiar that not only Fred Bellows didn't seem too upset about Tom Decker's death, but also the other two guys didn't seem that upset either. He kept wondering about what was going on and why the detective was so interested in Fred. Maybe the cops always acted this way when there was a death from an accident. He decided to watch and listen more carefully in the next couple of days to see if he could gather any other strange actions by any of his friends. His thoughts were momentarily interrupted as he thought he heard the garage door open. He guessed someone was putting their car in the garage which seemed a strange thing to do this time of day.

He tried to recall some of the things he heard different people say and some of their reactions. He already told Debbie what Ginger Bellows said about putting more money in land. He vaguely remembered something that Pam said about not liking gambling or living in Reno. He also thought about Pam's reaction when she learned about the money. She was elated and started jumping around. Debbie, his wife, reacted the same way, happy and glad about the winnings. The rest of the group seemed to be subdued and somewhat hesitant about showing their elated emotions.

Maybe they are not so elated, he thought. *But why not? Suddenly knowing that you have over a million dollars coming to you is something to get excited about. But why doesn't anyone want to tell anyone about it? They don't even want their kids to know.*

As George lay there, he kept thinking about the situation but could not find any answers to his mental questions.

CHAPTER 21

As George was thinking about the day's events, Dave Wheeler was standing at his upstairs bedroom window looking out at the ocean. He glanced down and noticed the Jacuzzi that was in the deck directly below his bedroom. He stared at the Jacuzzi for a long while. He began to think of a plan that might help him get more money from the lottery ticket.

If one couple is eliminated, that means we get over three hundred thousand more. For that kind of money I bet I could get the other couples to swear that the departed couple never put their money in the lottery ticket pot, so their family would not get any of the money.

He stood there looking at the Jacuzzi thinking through his newly conceived plan. He was familiar with electricity and was fairly handy around the house. His mind went through a scenario that he believed he could get away with. He thought of questions that may be asked and what activities he could put in place to answer any questions that may come up. After trying to think the plan through several times, he decided then it would work. He turned and said to his wife Norma who was lying on the bed reading, "I'm going downstairs for a little while. I don't want to stay up here while the sun is shining."

Norma didn't say anything as Dave walked out of the room. He remembered that Pam's car was in the garage when she pulled out, which meant that there was a spot for another car. Dave went to the garage, opened the door then drove his car in. He released the trunk and went to the back of his car. He was glad that he took the option to have a standard size spare tire when he bought the car. He unscrewed the holding cap and lifted the tire out of its holding area. He had the dealer rotate his tires about a month ago. He always rotated five tires, which included the spare, rather than four. He figured if he always rotated five tires he would get more miles from his tires. He put the spare tire on the ground, re-screwed the holder back in place, and put the tire in his trunk. He looked around for the toolbox that the rental house left for the renters, which had a few tools available. He found the toolbox, picked up a hammer and searched for a nail. He found a box of nails in the toolbox, pulled one out and walked back to his trunk. He drove the nail in the spare tire and stood there while the air leaked out, making the tire flat.

He closed his trunk, put the hammer back and thinking about it, wiped the hammer handle clean of any finger prints. He looked for a screwdriver but did not see one. He remembered that in his trunk was a small cloth holder that had some tools in it. He went back to his trunk, opened it and found the small tool bag. He took out a screwdriver and with the masking tape he found in the tool box, taped the metal end of the screw driver. He put the screwdriver on the shelf next to the electrical outlet. He looked around the garage and spotted the extension cord that he had picked up the night before and wanted to make sure it was in the same place that he left it. Satisfied, he opened the door between the garage and the house and went inside.

He stopped just inside the garage door and hesitated. He turned around and went back into the garage and once again opened his trunk. He remembered that he had never needed to change a tire before so the jack and tire iron were still brand new. He took out the flat spare tire and unlocked the jack and the tire iron. Walking outside, he took both the tools he had taken out of his trunk and put them in the dirt. He pushed on them and moved them back and forth so they would get scratched. Satisfied, he put the jack and the tire iron back in his trunk, along with the spare tire, closed the trunk and once again walked back into the house.

Once inside the house, Dave looked around to see if anyone had come down from their rest. Seeing no one, he walked over and picked up a portable radio that Fred and Ginger Bellows had brought to be used for background music during their stay at Russell Cove. Dave took the radio and walked out to the Jacuzzi and looked for the closest electrical outlet. He found one not too far from the Jacuzzi and plugged in the radio. As he suspected, the end of the radio cord had a small transformer and when plugged into the wall socket, covered the two-pronged outlet. This outlet had the GFCI electrical safety interrupter installed, but was covered up when the radio was plugged in. He sat the radio back away from the Jacuzzi and returned to the bedroom where Norma was lying on the bed reading.

"What have you been doing? Your hands are all dirty," she said as she looked up from her book.

"I was restless and wanted to do something so I cleaned up the garage. I want to be a good renter," he responded as he walked into the bathroom to wash his hands.

"I've been trying to read to get the accident out of my mind, but it's very difficult to do," she said.

"I know," responded Dave. "I feel the same way and have been thinking about it all day. What a terrible thing to have happened."

"I hope Pam is all right driving down to San Francisco," Norma said.

"She seemed OK when she left, and when she sees her son, things will start to look better."

"It's almost wine time," she said. "After the day we've had I'm sure everyone will be ready for some wine."

"I'm sure they will be," he responded, thinking about the Jacuzzi.

CHAPTER 22

The group started gathering in the living room, somewhat rested from their time alone. The room was rather quiet as each seemed to be lost in their own thoughts. Everyone was dressed for dinner except Fred and Ginger Bellows. They had their bathing suits on with robes over them.

"I'll open some wine," Dave Wheeler yelled from the kitchen to the group. "In fact I'll put it in the wine chiller so it will remain cold while we drink it."

Jim Schroeder eyed the wine bottle and thought of the cyanide pills. He quickly put the thought out of his head as there was no way to do anything with the group and get away with out being a suspect.

Maybe at dinner, but I doubt it, he thought as he took a glass of wine from Dave.

"Pam must be at the airport by now," mentioned Debbie.

"I hope she got there OK as she was pretty shaken up," said Fred Bellows.

"I still think we were crazy letting her go by herself," said Ginger Bellows.

Dave Wheeler was looking at Ginger's legs as her robe fell open. *Still a good looking woman,* he thought.

George and Debbie Mitchell sat on the couch, and George watched the others as they started to drink their wine. After a few minutes he got up and poured himself and Debbie a glass.

"Fred, why do you think the detective was asking you all those questions?" George asked.

"What do you mean by 'all those questions'?" Fred responded somewhat defensively.

"Well, he was asking you about handling the clubs and the golf ball. It seemed he questioned if Tom's neck could be broken by the golf cart. You recall that he asked that of Jim when he found out he was a doctor."

"Think what you want to George. I was clear up on the other side of the fairway when the cart tipped over. Other golfers saw me and told the detective that. How could I have been any way involved if I was not near the cart when it tipped over? What are you implying?"

"Calm down Fred," George said. "I was just wondering why the detective acted the way he did."

"I expect to get a call any time now from Detective Morrison telling me that my gear is coming back. I'm sure he will tell me the death was determined to be a terrible accident. What the hell else could it be?"

"What time are we going for dinner?" remarked Debbie Mitchell, trying to break the mood and change the subject.

"I'm ready any time," said Dave Wheeler as he looked as his wife Norma for agreement.

"Well, have as good a time as you can, with all that has happened today," said Ginger. "Fred and I will just stay here and munch on a few things and sit in the Jacuzzi and relax and drink some wine."

Fred went out on the deck and started the Jacuzzi.

The other three couples got up ready to leave. They all went back to their rooms to get their personal things and to freshen up. When Dave Wheeler reached his room he picked up the tape of *The Birds* that they had watched the night before. He put it under his coat that he had draped over his arm and walked back into the living room. Everyone else was there waiting for him.

"I'll drive," said Dave. "I don't think we need to take two cars."

"We can squeeze three couples in our car," responded Norma. "We're not going far anyway."

"You all have a good time at dinner," Ginger said again. Fred didn't say anything as he acted like he was still upset with George.

Fred and Ginger Bellows walked the three couples to the door and watched them leave.

"Do you think George thinks you had something to do with Tom's accident?" Ginger asked her husband as they walked back toward the Jacuzzi.

I don't think it would be a good idea to tell her the truth at this time, he thought. "I don't know what George was getting at, but I'll tell you that I had nothing to do with what happened up there on the golf course."

"I don't understand what the detective is thinking," she responded. "What possible reason would you have to harm Tom?"

"I don't know either. Let's pour some wine, get in the Jacuzzi and relax for awhile."

Fred went out to the deck and checked the Jacuzzi. He came back in the house and picked up two wine glasses and opened up a bottle of white wine. He poured a glass for Ginger as she was sitting on the deck with her robe on waiting for the Jacuzzi to get hot.

"I feel terrible about Tom, but so much better now about our financial situation. That million dollars is going to come in real handy," Ginger said to Fred as they were sitting on the deck. "We can relax now, pay off our bills and wait for the land to sell. Don't you agree that things are much better?"

"I guess so," responded Fred. "We had a four million dollar net worth some months ago. One million might hold us a while, but we need to build on it to really be safe." *I have to start thinking about how to get rid of another couple,* Fred thought. *We don't have much time before someone tells someone about the ticket, and then it will be too late. I'll see what I can think up while we're sitting in the Jacuzzi. I have to think of something and do it fast.*

Fred went over and checked the temperature of the water. He motioned to his wife to come on over as he climbed into the water. Ginger walked over, put her wine glass on the side and slipped in the water with Fred.

"Isn't that our radio?" she said to Fred as she pointed to the radio that was sitting on the side table next to the Jacuzzi.

"It looks like it," Fred said.

"How did it get out here?"

"I don't know. Obviously someone was going to listen to it, I guess."

They thought it was rather strange, but neither one of them thought any more about it.

Once they were in the Jacuzzi, Fred's thoughts turned to their relationship.

"Should we take off our swim suits?" he said to Ginger.

"I don't think so. What if they come back early and we're sitting here nude?"

"Come on Ginger. They just left and will be gone for at least an hour. You know how I like to sit with you in a Jacuzzi without clothes on."

"I would feel too uncomfortable," she responded.

"Well, if you don't want to take off the whole suit, how about at least dropping the top down?"

"I don't know. What if someone comes in?"

"It's a one piece suit. You can quickly pull the top back up. You know how I enjoy looking at your body. You know how I enjoy caressing your breasts," Fred said moving closer to her.

"Fred, this is crazy. I will drop the top of my suit, but you stay on the other side of the Jacuzzi."

"Come on Ginger that's not fair. After the kind of day I've had, a little love and care would do me good," Fred said with a pained look on his face.

"I know you, Fred Bellows. If you agree to stay on your side of the Jacuzzi, I'll drop my top."

"OK, OK," Fred relented and moved to the other side of the Jacuzzi. He stood their drinking his wine, enjoying both the taste of the liquid and the view of his wife's breasts.

CHAPTER 23

The three couples squeezed into Dave's car and not much was said on their way to dinner. When they arrived at the restaurant, everyone commented on how nice the day was and how pretty it was at the restaurant looking out over the ocean at Russell Cove. They all expressed their desire to have Tom and Pam Decker with them, but they knew that was not possible. They still could not believe Tom was dead.

Dave asked for a table for six and they were seated right away. As they sat down and started looking at the menu, Dave stood up and said, "I have the tape of *The Birds* in the car. I'll return it for you Jim so you will not get charged for two days."

"That's OK Dave," Jim responded, "I can take it back."

"I have my car, and the tape is in the front seat. I'll drop it in the return box as they are probably closed. You all go ahead and order some wine. I'll be back shortly."

Dave walked out to the parking lot, got into his car, and drove to the little house up the street that rented movies. He returned the tape in the slot provided for late returns. As he was walking back to his car, he pulled out his cell phone and called his wife Norma who was waiting in the restaurant.

"Dave?" she answered.

"I'm going to be a little later than I had planned," he told her. "I discovered one of my tires is flat, and I need to change it before I come back to the restaurant."

"Do you want me to call Triple A?" she asked.

"No, I have all the tools I need. I'll get it done and rejoin you in fifteen minutes or so. Besides, I'm not sure where Triple A would have to come from to get to the parking lot here in Russell Cove."

"OK, we'll sip our wine and wait for you."

Dave got back in his car and within a few minutes was in front of the rental house. He sat there for a couple of moments looking around to see if there was anyone out for their evening walk. He could not see anyone, and most of the houses were dark, which meant that they were probably unoccupied. He walked in the door and could hear the Jacuzzi running and some muted talking between Fred and Ginger. Dave walked to the garage, picked up the screwdriver with the taped edge. He walked to the main circuit box which was in the garage and jammed the screw driver in the main circuit breaker so it would remain closed. He picked up the extension cord and walked from the garage into the kitchen. He found the electric wine chiller that he had brought from home sitting on the kitchen cabinet. Putting the chiller under his arm and carrying the extension cord, he walked out to the deck where Fred and Ginger Bellows were relaxing in the Jacuzzi.

"Dave, what the hell, you scared me," Fred said somewhat startled as he noticed Dave coming out on the deck. Ginger was also startled as she had taken down the top of her bathing suit and had to quickly submerge herself up to her neck in the water.

"Don't mind me," Dave said as he noticed Ginger just before she ducked down in the water. "I know you two are relaxing, and I thought I would help you by keeping your wine chilled."

"We don't need to chill the wine. We only have a half bottle left and that will be gone soon," Fred replied.

Without saying anything, Dave plugged in the extension cord in the outlet on the other side of the deck and started toward the Jacuzzi. He noticed that Ginger had managed to slip up the top of her bathing suit. He took the wine chiller and plugged it into the extension cord and turned it on.

"I said we really don't need the wine chilled," replied Fred again, getting a little nervous.

Ignoring his comment, Dave moved to the Jacuzzi and picked up the half bottle of wine and put it in the chiller, which was making a slight vibrating noise.

"Sure you do. In fact this will chill the whole water," he said as he threw the chiller and the bottle into the water.

"What the hell…." Fred Bellows exclaimed which were his last words as he and Ginger both started to get out of the Jacuzzi. They didn't make it out before both of them screamed as the electricity surged through their bodies.

Dave didn't stay to watch but started back toward the house. He knew that within moments both of them would be dead. He went into the garage and pulled out the screwdriver that was holding the main circuit breaker closed. He had time enough to check to see if there were any scratch marks on the breaker before it snapped open and all the electricity went off in the house.

Dave got back in his car and sat there for a moment with his head back and eyes closed. He had a hard time believing what he had just done and kept telling himself he did it for himself and Norma. Taking a deep breath, he once again searched the area to see if anyone was around. He didn't know what he would do if he saw someone, but there was not anyone in sight. He started the car but turned it off and re-entered the garage. He picked up the screwdriver, opened the trunk. He unrolled the cloth holder that held his tools and placed the screwdriver back in its place. He once again looked around, started the car, and drove to the restaurant. He found an empty spot and parked in the lot. He got out, opened his trunk and ran his hands up and down the flat tire ensuring that his hands were dirty. Satisfied, he walked into the restaurant and moved to the table where the group was sitting drinking their wine.

"I'll be right back," he said. "I have to wash up as I got dirty changing the tire." After cleaning up, he rejoined the group and picked up his wine glass.

"Sorry it took me so long. But I had a little problem with the jack. I need a glass of wine," he mentioned. "Changing a tire is hard work so pass me the wine."

CHAPTER 24

The dinner conversation centered around the accident that Tom had that morning, and speculation about what Pam was going to do with her life now that Tom was gone. Everyone agreed that she would probably move back to Phoenix because she liked it there, and it was close to her son. The conversation eventually got around to the lottery money and what they were going to do with their winnings. About the time most of them were finished with their main course, George Mitchell's cell phone rang. He looked down at his phone, and it registered that the call was coming from Pam.

"It's Pam," George said as he flipped open the phone and started to walk away from the table.

"Be sure and tell her to let us know where she is staying tonight," Debbie responded.

George looked at Debbie and nodded his head, walked away and pushed the talk button. "How was the drive to San Francisco?" George said as he pushed the talk button.

"Is this Mr. Decker?" a male voice responded.

Taken back a little, George hesitated then questioned, "Who are you?"

"Please answer my question, sir."

"No, I'm not Tom Decker. Why are you on Pam Decker's phone?"

"Are you a friend or relative of Mrs. Decker?" the voice asked.

"Yes, I'm a family friend. Why are you asking and why are you on Pam's phone."

"My name is Cory Hanson. I'm with the California Highway Patrol, and your number was in the 'In Case of Emergency' contacts on Mrs. Decker's cell phone."

"Yes, we put it in her phone this afternoon before she left for San Francisco. Has something happened?"

"I'm sorry to inform you that Mrs. Decker had an accident going south on Highway 101 this afternoon."

"Is she all right? Was she hurt?"

"She lost control of her vehicle, rolled over a few times, and was hit by a large truck. She was killed instantly."

"Holy shit," George mumbled.

"What's happened? What's wrong?" Debbie and Linda said almost in unison as they were looking at George even though he was standing a few feet from the table.

"One moment officer," George said as he put his hand over the phone. He walked back to the table and said, "Pam's been killed in a car accident," he told the group at the table. He took his hand from the phone, put it up to his ear, and continued to talk to the patrol officer. "She was driving to San Francisco to pick up her son who was coming into the airport to meet her. Her husband was killed this morning in a golf cart accident."

"My God," Officer Hanson whispered. After a moment's hesitation he asked a question. "Do you have her son's phone number?"

"His name is Taylor Decker, and his home phone is in her phone but not his cell phone. That's why my number was there. I'm sure he will be waiting at the airport and wondering what happened because she is not there to pick him up."

"Where does he live?" the officer asked

"He's coming in from Phoenix," George responded.

"I see on her phone there are some missed calls, and the indication is there is a message for her. I believe I can contact him at this number. It has a 480 area code that I believe is the area code for the Phoenix area. Thank you sir, if I have trouble contacting him I'll page him at the airport. If that fails, I may call you back to see if you can be of further service. Where are you located?"

"We're in Russell Cove, and you obviously have my number."

"Thank you, and again I'm sorry about your friend."

The group sat around the table with stunned looks on their faces. The three ladies started to ask questions about how it happened, where it happened, did someone hit her, where was Taylor, what were they going to do now, and a bunch of other unanswerable questions.

"We'll find out the answers to these questions in due time. Right now I think we should go back to the house and wait there. Maybe Taylor is trying to contact us, and we should be there for him. We also need to let Fred and Ginger know, if they have not already talked to Taylor," George said as he waved to the waiter to bring them their check.

The six of them returned to Dave's car and started back to the house. It was getting dark, and as they approached the house, Jim noticed that all the lights were out.

"Maybe Fred and Ginger stepped out," Dave Wheeler said knowing what they were going to find on the deck of the house.

"They told us that they were going to stay put and relax and have some wine," Jim's wife Linda Schroeder responded.

Dave drove in the driveway, parked the car, and everyone got out. George was the first one in the front door and confirmed to everyone else that all the electricity was out.

"Do you have a flash light in your car?" George asked Dave.

"Yes," he responded. "I'll get it."

As they waited for Dave to get his flashlight, Jim called out "Fred –Ginger," and received no response. "Where is the main circuit?" he asked the group.

"I think it's in the garage," responded Dave.

Dave gave Jim the flashlight and watched as Jim found his way through the garage and opened the cover over the fuse box.

"The main circuit breaker is open," Jim called back. He tried to close it but it kept snapping open. "Something's wrong," Jim said. "The breaker will not stay closed."

"I found another flashlight here in the kitchen," George Mitchell yelled. "I'll look out back to see if Fred and Ginger are here. Jim, why don't you look upstairs in their bedroom." Jim left the garage and walked upstairs.

George walked out to the deck. He noticed an extension cord that was plugged in the wall. It ran to the Jacuzzi and disappeared in the water. George knew the electricity was out so he walked over to the outlet and unplugged the extension cord.

"Jim, try closing the breaker now," he yelled inside the house.

"Jim's upstairs," Dave responded. "I'll see if I can find it and throw the switch." Dave knew where the fuse box was, walked out in the garage, found the box, and flipped on the main circuit breaker. This time it stayed closed and the electricity was restored.

George walked over and turned on the deck lights. He once again looked at the extension cord that disappeared in the Jacuzzi. He thought he knew what he would find when he looked in the Jacuzzi. He breathed deeply and walked over to the Jacuzzi and looked down inside. What he saw made him sick. At the bottom were both Fred and Ginger Bellows, looking up at him with their eyes open and grotesque looks on their faces. George turned his head, stood there for a moment, then ran to the side of the deck, and threw up his dinner.

Jim came out on the deck, saw what George was doing, and asked, "George, you all right?"

"Fred and Ginger are both dead, call 911," he said.

Jim stood there; he looked at the extension cord and followed it with his eyes to the Jacuzzi. He walked over and saw both the bodies in the bottom.

"Jesus!" he exclaimed. He took out his cell phone and dialed 911.

CHAPTER 25

After Detective Morrison left the Medical Examiner and went back to his office, he kept thinking about the golf cart and the accident. The main thing that did not fit in the puzzle was the motive. He knew there was something that someone was not telling him. He called one of his investigator contacts in Sacramento and told him about what happened on the golf course. He asked his friend to see what he could find out about Fred Bellows in the next couple of hours. He didn't want a full investigation yet but thought maybe something would turn up with a quick look.

It wasn't long before his contact called him back and told him that Fred Bellows was in some kind of land deal that went sour. According to his sources, the number of twelve million dollars was kicked around. There were three people who bought the land anticipating a quick sale to a developer, but due to some kind of Indian artifacts that were discovered on the land, it became untouchable and was now just sitting there.

Detective Morrison thanked his friend and hung up the phone. So, there was the possibility of a financial problem in the Bellows' house.

How would it benefit Bellows to kill Decker? Decker lived in Reno. Maybe he was one of the three who invested in the land deal.

He kept reviewing all the ramifications that he could think of relative to what a motive could be. He decided to close the office and go home to have some dinner. Before he left he called Larry Gravits and asked him how the autopsy was coming. Gravits told him it would still be another hour or so before it was complete. Detective Morrison asked Gravits to call him at home when he reached his conclusion.

He closed the office, went home, greeted Pearl, and tried to relax before dinner. He talked to Pearl about his experience that day and about some of the things that were puzzling him relative to the case. She knew that he would become obsessed with this case until it was solved. He often talked to her about his thoughts as she was a good listener and sometimes had some good ideas about the various situations.

"Is this Fred guy a serial killer?" Pearl asked her husband as she was putting together the salad for dinner.

"No. In fact as far as I know he as never been in trouble before," he responded.

"You told me once, Wilt, that there are generally only two reasons people kill people, either for love or money."

"I still believe that," Detective Morrison said.

"Well, if you can't find where any money is involved, is Fred, or whatever his name is, having an affair with the wife of the guy he killed?" she asked.

"There is no indication of that, but who knows. I haven't been around any of them long enough to find out."

"Well it's probably one or the other, and I'd bet there is some strong emotion that will come to play here. Dinner's about ready. Are you ready?"

Detective Morrison continued to think about what Pearl said through dinner. The conversation shifted to Pearl's discovery of how bad people's teeth were and how easy it is to prevent tooth disease.

It was an hour later when Larry Gravits called about the autopsy. The same time that George and Jim found Fred and Ginger Bellows in the Jacuzzi at the rental house, Detective Wilt Morrison was talking on the phone to Larry Gravits, the medical examiner. Larry had worked overtime doing the autopsy on Tom Decker and was reporting the results to Detective Morrison.

"There is no question that he died from a broken neck," Larry went on. "We know about the bruise on the side of his head. What else I found was there were some slight bruises around the bottom of his ears and on his lower jaw. It looks like someone pulled on his head pretty strong or gave his head a twist."

"Did the roll-over kill him or was it something or someone else?" Morrison asked.

"It's hard to tell for sure, but if I were a betting man I would say he was already dead when the cart turned over. There were some small cuts on his arms where the rock scratched him on the roll-over that should have caused more bleeding. I would say the blood had started to coagulate before the roll-over."

"That's good enough for me. I think I will pay another visit to Fred Bellows this evening. I'd like to go over his story with him one more time to see if he changed anything. I'll contact the DA tomorrow and let her know what is going on, and I'm sure she will agree with me that we have enough to arrest this guy for murder, or at the very least bring him in for questioning."

"OK. In the meantime I will continue to look at the dirt samples on the driver and compare them to the dirt on the cart's accelerator. I think we might have this guy nabbed."

"The one question still in my mind," Morrison continued, "what is the motive? Why would someone kill one of his best friends at this time after they have been coming here for all these years?"

"Dig deep enough, and you will find something. I'm out of here. Talk to you later."

Detective Morrison looked at his watch. It was getting late, and he wondered if he should go over to the rental house tonight or wait until in the morning. He pondered for a few moments and decided that Fred Bellows would be there in the morning. He would pick him up before he had a chance to eat breakfast. He started to get undressed for bed when the phone rang.

"Morrison," he said as he picked up the phone.

"Detective Morrison, I'm William Anderson, the paramedic out at Russell Cove. I wanted you to know that we had another accident out here this evening, and two people died."

"What happened?"

"It seems that a man and his wife were sitting in the Jacuzzi drinking wine when the electric wine chiller fell into the water. They were electrocuted."

"Jesus," mumbled Detective Morrison. *The tourists coming up here are getting dumber and dumber,* he thought. "William, you are going to have to call the office and get another detective to look at this one. I've got a case this morning that I'm working on and don't have time to get into something else."

"I know you are working on the golf cart accident that happened this morning, but I think you will have time to look into this one."

"What do you mean?" Detective Morrison said.

"The guy you are investigating for the golf cart accident was in the Jacuzzi. He's dead."

"You talking about Fred Bellows?'

"Yes. I was there this morning on the golf course when you came down. Apparently Mr. Bellows and his wife got into the Jacuzzi this evening rather than joining the others for dinner. That's when it happened."

"Who discovered the bodies?"

"When the three couples came home, they noticed the electricity was off. When they got it back on, they found the bodies in the bottom of the Jacuzzi."

"Have you removed the bodies from the Jacuzzi?"

"We always remove a body from the water because we are never sure if the person or persons have been in the water for a long time or just a few minutes before we get to the scene. We can't take the chance that they are not still alive or can be resuscitated."

"I have a thousand other questions. I'll get dressed and come on over. Tape off the scene and keep everyone there in the house. I'll be there in about a half an hour."

Detective Morrison put back on his work clothes and headed for the door. He told Pearl he would be late and mentioned what the phone call was about. As he pulled out of the driveway, he put in a call to Larry Gravits.

When Larry answered, Detective Morrison said, "Forget about any further investigation of the Tom Decker case."

"Why, what happened?"

"I just got a call from the paramedics. They found Fred Bellows and his wife at the bottom of a Jacuzzi. Apparently they were electrocuted. I think you best come over to the house and meet me there so we can see for ourselves what is going on."

He gave Larry the address. Larry agreed to meet there as soon as he got cleaned up and could drive over.

Detective Morrison was still puzzled about what was going on.

CHAPTER 26

After Jim Schroeder called the paramedics from the deck, he and George went into the rental house to talk to the wives. They had both agreed not to let the wives go out to the deck and see the bodies inside the Jacuzzi. Neither of them expected the reaction they received when they explained that there had been an accident, and both Fred and Ginger were dead. The news of the morning about Tom, then the accident with his wife Pam, and now this was overwhelming for Jim Schroeder's wife Linda. She started crying and moaning uncontrollably. It looked like she was going to faint. Although extremely distraught about the news, the other two women were more worried about Linda and gathered around her trying to calm her down.

"I have some sedatives upstairs," Jim mentioned. "Let me get her up to the bedroom and see if I can get her to take something to get her calmed down."

With that he half carried Linda up the stairs to their bedroom. Jim told Linda to lie down on the bed. He went to his small medical bag and took out some strong sleeping pills and gave one to Linda. He started to put them back in his bag when he thought he would probably give his wife some more pills later. He put the vile of pills in the medicine cabinet behind the bathroom mirror. Jim stayed in the room with Linda for a few minutes. When she calmed down and seemed to relax, he went back downstairs.

For the next fifteen minutes the conversation between George and Debbie Mitchell and Dave and Norma Wheeler centered on how they could not believe what was happening to their group. All but Dave were in a half state of shock. George still felt sick to his stomach for what he had seen on the deck.

The paramedics arrived and took charge. They took the bodies out of the Jacuzzi and placed them on the deck. After they were certain the pair were dead, they put sheets over them. One of the paramedics called Detective Morrison at his home. After the phone conversation, the paramedic told the group that the detective was on his way over and for none of them to touch anything on the deck and wait for the detective to arrive.

Twenty minutes later the doorbell rang, and rather than waiting for someone to answer the door, Detective Morrison walked in. He walked through the house heading for the deck. As he walked by the five people sitting in the living room, he didn't speak but nodded his head to two of the men who looked up at him. He went out to the deck and started to take in the scene. He noticed the two bodies lying on the deck with sheets over them. He spent a few minutes talking to the two paramedics. He walked back in the house, looked at the group, and could see that the women were very distressed. The men were sitting there with blank stares on their faces.

"Who can tell me what happened?" he asked.

"We came back to the house from dinner and found Fred and Ginger in the Jacuzzi," George Mitchell responded.

"Who was at dinner?" asked Detective Morrison.

"We all were," responded Dave Wheeler.

"What time did you leave and where did you go?" Detective Morrison wanted to know.

Jim Schroeder spoke up and told the detective about what time they left and where they went. He explained that when they returned, the electricity was off. They had to find flashlights so they could look around. He continued to tell the detective that Dave Wheeler located the main circuit box in the garage. Jim said that he tried to close the circuit but it kept opening. That's when George Mitchell saw the extension cord plugged in on the deck, unplugged it and the breaker stayed closed. It was then that the lights came on.

"I saw the cord leading to the Jacuzzi and found Fred and Ginger at the bottom. I wish I would never have looked."

"George was throwing up over the deck rail when I came out. I saw the bodies and called 911," said Jim Schroeder.

Detective Morrison walked back out on the deck to take a closer look at what happened. He walked over to the Jacuzzi and looked inside. There was a wine chiller at the bottom of the tank. There was also a wine bottle and two wine glasses lying on the bottom. He saw an extension cord running from the wine chiller back to an outlet on the other side of the deck. Detective Morrison put on his gloves and walked over to the outlet and noticed it was unplugged. He walked over to the radio that was plugged into a wall socket next to the Jacuzzi. He noticed that the radio was plugged in, and the transformer covered the two outlets. He unplugged the radio and saw there was a GFCI circuit breaker installed in the outlet. He plugged the radio back in and turned it on. There was faint music coming from the sound but it the volume was fairly low and there was lots of static on the station.

If they were listing to the radio while they were in the Jacuzzi the volume is so low and the reception so poor they could not hear it above the sound of the air jets, he thought.

He unplugged the radio and was puzzled for a moment as the sound kept coming out. *This radio has batteries in it.* He turned up the volume to a sufficient level where he concluded the batteries were still good. He walked back in the house and looked at the group.

"Who was it who found the bodies in the Jacuzzi?" he asked.

"I did," responded George Mitchell.

"Was the radio playing when you came out on the deck?" he asked.

George thought a minute and said that he did not remember hearing the radio.

"Who did the radio belong to?" Detective Morrison asked.

"It belonged to Fred and Ginger Bellows. They brought it to the rental house to listen to background music when we were eating or sitting around talking," George answered.

"The radio probably went off when the electricity went off," said Dave Wheeler. "What's important about that?"

"If the radio is unplugged, the radio works off the batteries. It was their radio, and they knew it had batteries in it. The radio was still plugged in the outlet. I don't think they were listening to the radio as the volume was too low."

"I don't understand," said Dave

"Well, Mr. ah, Wheeler is it?" Detective Morrison when on, "The wine chiller was plugged into an outlet without a circuit breaker. The outlet was clear across the deck. These two people were not stupid. They probably knew about the danger of having something electric around the Jacuzzi, particularly if it were plugged into an outlet with no circuit breaker. Why didn't they play the radio using the batteries, and plug the wine chiller into the outlet closer to them?"

"Maybe they were still upset about what happened this morning to Tom Decker and weren't thinking straight," Dave said as he turned his eyes away from the detective.

"Maybe," Detective Morrison said, noticing Dave Wheeler's reaction and his body language. "Were they in the Jacuzzi when you all left for dinner?"

George thought a moment then answered, "No, they walked to the door and watched us leave. They must have gone into the Jacuzzi after we left."

Detective Morrison went back out to the deck and studied the extension cord and the wine chiller. He tried to visualize the wine chiller sitting on the side of the Jacuzzi and where it would be located. He looked at the present location of the wine chiller and could not come to any conclusions. He surmised that no matter where the chiller fell into the Jacuzzi the air jets could have moved it around until the electricity shut off. He also thought about the wine bottle and the two glasses.

No telling how much wine was in the bottle, he thought. *And it is going to be difficult to get fingerprints off the wine chiller, the glass bottle and glasses because of the hot water and how long they had been at the bottom.* While he was thinking about that situation, the medical examiner walked out to the deck.

"I don't think there's much question about the cause of death," Detective Morrison told Larry Gravits.

While Larry started looking over the two bodies, Detective Morrison walked back in the house to address the group.

"You all went to dinner together, isn't that what you told me?" he asked.

"Yes we did," responded George.

"Were you all together there the whole time?"

"Well, no," George said as he looked over at Dave Wheeler. "Dave left for awhile to return the movie we rented last night."

"Where did you return the movie, and how long were you gone?" Detective Morrison asked as he looked over at Dave.

Dave told him where he had delivered the video. He continued,

"I discovered I had a flat tire when I was about to get back in my car from putting the video in the night box. I called my wife Norma from the parking lot. I told her about the tire. I told her that I needed to change it and would be later getting back to dinner."

"That's correct detective," Norma added. "He did call me and told me about the tire."

"What time was that?" Detective Morrison asked.

"Probably around six thirty," Dave answered.

"Did anyone see you in the lot changing your tire?" asked Detective Morrison.

"I don't know. I think there were a couple of cars that came by and returned videos or DVD's, but I didn't pay any attention to them."

"Could you recognize their cars or what they looked like?" Detective Morrison asked.

"No, I told you that I was so busy changing my tire that I didn't pay any attention to them."

"It would be hard not to notice a man in that small parking lot changing a tire," Detective Morrison added. "It would help if someone saw you there. I'll call the owner tonight and ask him to hold any DVD's or tapes that were returned in the late box. We can get the names from the returns and follow up to see if anyone remembers seeing you."

Shit, Dave thought. "I don't know if they were returning tapes or not," Dave said. "And there were only maybe one or two cars at the most. I don't really know as I was busy with my tire. They could have been just turning around, I really don't know."

Why does he keep changing his story? He also looks nervous as hell, Detective Morrison thought.

"Do you think my husband has something to do with this?" Norma Wheeler said.

"I don't know," Detective Morrison responded. "All I know at this point is two people are dead from an electric wine chiller falling into the Jacuzzi. One of them had to find the extension cord and the wine chiller, plug it into a wall socket away from where they were relaxing while listing to a radio that probably was not on. Then one of them had to knock the wine chiller into the Jacuzzi. It is possible, of course, but not probable in my mind."

"My husband had nothing to do with any of this. He was with us, and the only time he left he had a flat tire and that's what took him so long."

"I have to cover all the angles and answer all the questions that my boss and the insurance company will ask. I am just covering all the possible angles here," Detective Morrison said. He turned to Dave and continued. "Since you didn't have time to have your tire fixed I assume it is still in your trunk?"

"Yes," Dave said.

"Mind if I take a look at it?"

"Don't you need a warrant or something?" Dave added.

"I can get a warrant if I need one, but if you give me your permission, I can look at it now and avoid any impression of you being uncooperative."

"OK, OK, you can look at it. My car is right out front."

They both walked out to Dave's car. He opened the trunk, and Detective Morrison looked at the tire. He noticed it had been on the car previously.

"Mind pulling the tire out of the trunk?" he said

Dave reached in and pulled out the tire. "There is a nail in it. I noticed it last night when I was changing it. I must have run over it on the way to returning the video."

Detective Morrison looked around the trunk. He noticed a small rolled up tool carrier with a ribbon tied around it.

"Would you untie this tool carrier please," he asked Dave.

Dave untied the tool carrier and opened it so the detective could see that all it held were tools. Detective Morrison looked at the tools and saw a hammer, some pliers, a small flash light and a screwdriver with tape around the blade.

"I'd like to take a look at the jack and the tire iron please," Detective Morrison asked.

Dave reached in and took out the jack and the tire iron.

Detective Morrison looked at them both and noticed they had scratches on them as if they had been used. "I'll need to take the jack with me for a day," he said.

"Why?" asked Dave.

"Well, the parking lot at the video store is asphalt," responded Detective Morrison. "I'm going to have the lab look at the scratches on the jack and see if we can detect any bits of asphalt. That would be one less piece of the puzzle if we can find asphalt on this jack."

Shit, Dave thought again. "Sure take it. Just because you may not find asphalt bits doesn't prove anything. They could have fallen off when I put the jack in the car, or never attached themselves to the jack in the first place."

Detective Morrison didn't say anything. He put the jack in his car being very careful to ensure the bottom of the jack didn't touch anything. *He's right, but I need to have this guy worry over this situation,* he thought. He walked back into the garage and went over to the main fuse box. He wondered why the main circuit breaker didn't snap open as soon as the wine chiller hit the water. He thought that it would have happened so quickly that perhaps it would have saved their lives. He opened the cover to the box and examined the main circuit breaker. He could not see were anything was out of the ordinary. There were no scratches or marks on or around the breaker.

Detective Morrison was returning to the house as Larry Gravits and the paramedics were bringing out the bodies.

"I'm done here," Gravits said. "There's no question in my mind what they died of, but we'll do the autopsies as required. I'll let you know sometime tomorrow when I'm finished if there is anything else."

"Thanks, Doc," Detective Morrison said.

Detective Morrison walked back into the house where all five of the individuals were still sitting in the living room. He noticed Mrs. Wheeler looked at him with a sign of disgust, and then she looked away. George and Debbie Mitchell were sitting close together, and he was consoling her. Dave was sitting across the room next to his wife, and Dr. Jim Schroeder was sitting in a chair across from George.

"Just a couple more questions," Detective Morrison said. "I'm taking the extension cord to the lab with me. Whose finger prints will I find on it?"

"You'll find mine," George responded. "I pulled the plug from the wall so we could get the lights back on."

"Mine will also be on the cord," Dave said. "I was carrying it around last night as I plugged in the wine chiller during dinner. I suspect you will also find Fred's as he had to handle it to plug it in the wall." *I hope every thing is too smeared to tell as I don't think Fred's prints will be on the cord,* Dave thought.

"I don't see Mrs. Decker," Detective Morrison said. "I need to tell her that her husband's remains are available and where she can pick them up."

Debbie Mitchell looked at the detective and said in a voice that started to cry, "Pam Decker had a car accident this afternoon and was killed."

"What?" Detective Morrison said.

George Mitchell continued, "She was driving to San Francisco to pick up her son and had an accident this side of the tunnel just before the bridge. Apparently she lost control of her car and was hit by a large truck. She was dead at the scene."

What the hell is going on here? That's four people dead in one day, all from the same friendly group, Detective Morrison thought.

"How did you find out about the accident?"

"I put my number in her cell phone under the In Case of Emergency number to call. The highway patrol called me and informed me that she had the accident."

"Why was your number under the ICE description and not her husband's, or her son's?" Detective Morrison asked.

"Well," George went on. "We thought she needed an ICE number as she didn't have one in her phone. As her husband was killed this morning and she didn't know her son's cell number, I put my number in. She was supposed to change it when she got to her son at the airport."

"She didn't have her son's cell number? That's a little unusual," Detective Morrison said.

"Her son's number was changed recently. It was in her husband's phone, which you have, along with his golf clubs and other stuff," George said.

"Did they contact her son?" Detective Morrison asked.

"I assume they did," responded George. "I told the highway patrol officer to call me back if they had any problems. I haven't heard anything from them."

"What about any family members for the two individuals who were killed tonight?" Detective Morrison asked.

"Debbie looked up, eyes red from tearing and said, "They have a daughter who I think lives in the Denver area."

"Do you know her name?" Detective Morrison asked.

"It's Tammy Rapish, or Rappid, or something like that."

"Would you mind going through her things here in her room and see if you can find a number and a name for me?"

Debbie got up from where she was sitting and went upstairs to Fred and Ginger's room. She went in the room and hesitated at the door. She could not believe that they were both dead. It took her a minute to gather the courage to enter the room and look for an address book. She noticed clothes were thrown on the bed. Debbie assumed they were thrown there when Fred and Ginger were getting ready to go into the Jacuzzi. She looked around the room and saw Ginger's makeup bag. She looked in the bag and found an address book.

After Debbie left the living room, George looked at Detective Morrison and asked, "Do you really think that something is going on here and all these accidents were not accidents?"

"In my opinion there are too many things that don't add up about the accidents. Things like this just don't happen the way they're happening here. You're talking about four people killed in one day. Your group has been coming up here for years, and nothing even close to this has happened in the past. It's too much to be a coincidence. In fact I think I had enough information to take Mr. Bellows in for questioning tomorrow as I believe he killed Tom Decker."

"Damn," George said.

Detective Morrison continued. "Can any of you think of anything that has changed between all of you that was not there this time last year?"

George glanced at Dave, who very slightly shook his head signifying "no." Dave Wheeler knew that George was about to tell the detective about the lottery ticket. George thought for a moment and then didn't say anything.

"I can't think of anything," Jim Schroeder added. "There is still a possibility that these deaths were really an accident. So far nothing has been proven otherwise."

"Tom Decker's neck was broken by a strong twisting motion," Detective Morrison said losing his patience. "There were bruises on his chin which could indicate someone's fingers jerking his chin around. There was a bruise on the side of his head which could have come from a golf club. The dirt on the cover of the driver golf club matched the dirt on the accelerator of the golf cart. There was nothing found to be defective in the golf cart. Fred's finger prints were on Decker's golf ball and there were hairs from Tom Decker's head on Fred's driver."

All this isn't true but they don't know that, thought Detective Morrison.

"I personally think Fred Bellows killed Tom Decker for a reason that I don't know. Can any of you think of any reason why that would happen?"

No one said anything. The four of them just sat there and looked at each other.

Detective Morrison continued, "Now we have the death of Tom Decker's wife. I have no idea what happened, but I'm going to find out. If I were you, I would be concerned about who's next as it seems to me that it's not going to stop here. I also found out that Fred Bellows was in some kind of real estate deal that went sour. I think he was in trouble financially. That may have had something to do with his actions against Tom Decker."

About that time Debbie returned to the room carrying a piece of paper.

"I found the name and number," she said, handing the paper over to Detective Morrison. "Her name is Tammy Riley. She lives in Denver and her phone number is on the paper."

"Thank you. I'll contact her tonight and let her know what happened. I'll gather up some things from the deck. I would like you all to be here through tomorrow so we can get all this wrapped up. I assume none of you were planning to leave tomorrow?"

"No, we'll be here," responded George.

"Please write your home addresses on this piece of paper for me," he added as he gave each individual a piece of paper from his note book.

Detective Morrison went out to the deck, took some more pictures, gathered the extension cord, and put it in an evidence bag. He pulled the wine chiller, the wine bottle and both wine glasses out of the Jacuzzi and put them in evidence bags. He walked through the living room, collected the names and addresses from each individual and walked to his car and left.

CHAPTER 27

Taylor Decker stepped of the plane at the San Francisco airport and started walking toward the luggage area. Although he only brought a carry on bag with him, he knew that his mother would be waiting in that area. He could not believe that his father, Tom Decker, was killed earlier that day from a golf cart accident. He had gone through all kinds of emotions of shock and sorrow, and wanted to get the details from his mother.

Taylor was thirty-eight years old. He was just over six feet tall, and believed in keeping his body in good physical shape. He lifted weights and ran three miles almost every day. Taylor had a full head of light brown hair and deep brown eyes. He dressed very nicely and wore conservative clothes. He was employed as an insurance claim inspector for the Great Western Insurance Company. He started with this insurance company twelve years ago as a claims adjuster and worked his way up to be an investigator. He was good at his job, and well thought of in the company.

When he reached the luggage area he looked around for his mother, but didn't see her.

Maybe she's running a little late due to the traffic through the city, he thought. *I'll give her another few minutes then try her cell phone.*

He found a seat where he could sit and watch the door. His thoughts went back to the accident that his father had earlier that day. He knew he was going to miss his dad terribly. He hadn't seen much of either of his parents since they had moved to Reno. He talked to them about once a week on the phone and knew that his mother was not happy living in Reno, but being a dutiful wife had accepted the move. He once again felt a wave of sorrow flow through his body. He took a deep breath and tried to shake it off. He knew he had to be strong for his mother as she was going to count on his strength and guidance.

Taylor looked around the area once again, and still did not see his mother. He decided to call her cell phone to determine her location. He speed dialed her number and received only her voice mail asking to leave a recorded message. He left a message asking her to call him and let him know where she was. Puzzled, he wondered who else he could call that might know about her estimated time of arrival. He had the number of the rental house in Russell Cove. If he could talk to someone there maybe they could give him some information. He punched in the rental house number and listened to it ring nine times, then he hung up. Now he was getting worried.

He called his mother again and received the same response as before. He was wondering what his next move would be when his cell phone rang. He looked at the incoming number and saw his mother's name on the phone dial. Relieved, he answered the phone.

"Mom, where are you. I'm here at the airport."

He was surprised when a male voice answered him. "Are you Taylor Decker?" the voice asked.

"Yes," he responded. "Who are you and why do you have my mother's cell phone?"

"My name is Cory Hanson, Mr. Decker. I'm with the California Highway Patrol. I'm very sorry to inform you that your mother was killed this afternoon in a car accident as she was apparently coming to meet you at the airport."

All the blood seemed to drain out of Taylor's body. He couldn't say anything, and seemed to be having a difficult time breathing.

"I saw that you called her a few minutes ago. I talked to a Mr. George Mitchell, a friend of hers, and knew you were at the airport," Hanson continued.

"Give me a minute, please," Taylor managed to say. He knew if he didn't sit down he was going to faint. He walked over to a chair, sat down and put his head between his legs. After about thirty seconds he felt better and put the phone back to his ear.

"How did it happen?" he asked.

"It looks like she lost control in the fast lane. She hit the center divider and swerved back into traffic. A loaded semi hit her. She didn't have a chance."

There was another pause in the conversation before the highway patrol officer went on. "I understand you lost your father this morning. This has to be a nightmare for you. I'm so sorry to have to bring you this terrible news."

Taylor was trying to get his thoughts together, but was not having much success. He asked Hanson where her body was, and what they did with the car. He fumbled in his pocket and pulled out one of his business cards. He turned the card over and wrote down the name and address of where they had taken his mother. He also wrote down where they had taken the car.

"Officer, can you give me your phone number in case I need to contact you again? I'm not thinking very straight right now. I may think of something I forgot to ask later," Taylor said.

He took down the number, thanked the officer, and thought of something just before the conversation ended.

"You said you contacted George Mitchell about the accident. Why contact him, and how did you get his number?"

Cory Hanson explained about how George's number was in Pam's phone under the ICE contact. Taylor asked for the phone number, and after writing it down, thanked the officer and terminated the call.

Taylor sat there in the terminal for a few minutes thinking about his next move. He decided to call his wife and let her know what had happened. He thought that after he made the phone calls, he would rent a car, get a hotel, and try to get some rest. Tomorrow he would start picking up the pieces of what was left of his family.

About an hour later, Taylor was having trouble relaxing and decided to call George Mitchell. He opened his phone and punched in George Mitchell's number.

"This is George," the voice answered.

"Mr. Mitchell, this is Taylor Decker."

"Taylor, has the highway patrol contacted you?"

"Yes. I talked with Officer Hanson earlier this evening."

"This is unbelievable. Taylor, I can't tell you how sorry I am about what has happened today."

Taylor tried to remain professional. "Have they determined the cause of my dad's accident yet?" Taylor asked.

"I don't think so. I can give you the number of the detective who is working on clearing things up if you would like it."

"There is a detective working on this?" Taylor asked.

"Yes," responded George. "I'm told that is standard procedure when there is a death, even if is determined to be an accident."

"What else could it have been?" asked Taylor.

"Look, why don't you talk to the detective. He can give you the details. I'll give you his number."

Taylor took out another business card and wrote down the number.

"Look, if there is any thing Debbie and I can do to help, please let us know. We've been friends with your parents for many years. This whole thing is difficult for us too."

"I appreciate that," Taylor said. "I can't think if anything right now."

"I have your phone number now on my cell. Call us when you finalize your plans. We'll do whatever we can," George said.

"Thanks, George. I'll be in touch later," Taylor responded, said goodbye and flipped his phone shut.

CHAPTER 28

After the detective left, Jim went up to the room to check on his wife. George Mitchell and his wife Debbie were sitting in the living room with Dave and Norma Wheeler.

"Why didn't you want me to tell the detective about the lottery ticket?" George asked Dave.

"I just think it would complicate things right now. I'm sure it doesn't have any bearing on what is going on around here. If the detective knew about the ticket, he would have a lot more questions. He has enough now, in my opinion."

"You don't think the lottery ticket has any bearing on these events?" George commented.

"No I don't," said Dave. "Why should it? We all get over a million dollars and that alone should take care of us for the rest of our lives. I think what has happened with Tom, Pam, Fred and Ginger were terrible accidents. I think you have a detective who wants to make a name for himself and is trying to do everything he can to prove something that isn't there. Besides, I assume that we will split the money with the families of those that participated in buying the ticket so what purpose would it serve to eliminate anyone?"

"I'm not so sure about what you are saying," responded George. "Whether you like it or not, I'm going to tell the detective about the lottery ticket the next time I see him. I just don't feel right about hiding it any longer."

"Suit yourself George," Dave Wheeler said. "I think you're making a mistake but you need to do what you think is right." With that, Dave got up and asked Norma if she were ready for bed.

"I may be ready for bed, but I don't think I'm going to sleep very well. This has been a horrible day," she responded.

After Dave and Norma left the room, Jim Schroeder came back

down to the living room.

"Linda is sleeping soundly, which is good for her. She took the news of Fred and Ginger pretty bad."

"What do you think about telling the detective about the lottery ticket?" George asked Jim.

"I don't know. I don't think it has anything to do with what has happened here today. What do you think?"

"I don't know either, but I find it strange that no one wants to talk about it. I told Dave that the next time I see the detective I'm going to tell him. I'll let him decide if it means anything."

"What possible motive would anyone have to try and eliminate each other? I can see from all sides that what has happened today was nothing more that a couple of very unfortunate accidents."

George continued, "The detective sure seems to think otherwise."

"Think about it," Jim said. "First of all, Fred has two people that said he was nowhere near the golf cart when it tipped over. The cart could have rolled over on Tom and broken his neck. Fred could not have driven the cart down the hill, then rolled it over and run up the side of the golf course before the two other golfers saw him."

"But the detective said there were hairs from Tom on Fred's driver," responded George.

"We don't know that for sure. The detective could be telling us that just to get a reaction. Besides why would Fred want to hurt Tom? What possible motive would he have?"

"I don't know. What about Fred and Ginger? Don't' you think it's strange what happened to them?" George asked.

"Again, think about it. We didn't even know they were going to be in the Jacuzzi until late this afternoon. How could Dave have set that up? Do you think he went out and put a nail in his tire, then got all dirty just to cover his tracks?" Jim continued. "He didn't have time to think all that through. Once again, what possible motive would Dave have?"

"Fred and Ginger were smart people," George countered. "How could they be so stupid as to let the electric wine chiller fall into the water?"

"Everyone is distressed over what happened to Tom and Pam," Jim when on. "Maybe they just were not thinking clearly."

"They didn't even know about Pam's accident," Debbie Mitchell interjected. She had been quiet up until that point.

"No, but they knew about Tom, and Fred was there when it happened," Jim responded.

"What about Pam?" George continued. "That's another strange thing."

"We all know how distressed she was," Jim said. "It is possible that she was consumed with her thoughts and lost control of her car."

"I know we should not have let here drive in her condition," said Debbie.

"Don't blame yourself, Debbie," George said.

"It's been a terrible day but I think it all can be explained," Jim concluded. "I'm going up to bed as I need to be with Linda. See you all in the morning."

George and Debbie sat there for a few minutes after Jim left the room.

"Maybe he's right," George said. "But I'm still going to let the detective know about the lottery ticket. By the way, where is the ticket?"

Debbie thought for a moment and remembered, "Dave put it in his wallet this morning so I guess he still has it."

"OK, let's go upstairs and try and get some rest."

"I'm going to try and straighten up Fred and Ginger's room," Debbie responded. "When I went up to find their daughter's phone number I saw that they had clothes scattered all over the room. Someone has to get their things organized."

"Can't you do that in the morning?" George asked.

"I'll do it now as I can't sleep anyway. Someone also has to get Tom and Pam's things together. Maybe I'll do that in the morning."

They started to walk upstairs when George's cell phone rang. He answered it and told Debbie in a hushed voice "Taylor Decker." George continued on into his room. Debbie walked into Fred and Ginger's room. She stood there just looking at their things for a moment. Tears once again began to cover her eyes as she thought of the good times she and Ginger had enjoyed over the years. She started to fold their clothes, separated them, and put them on the unmade bed. She found their suitcases and put things as neatly as she could in each case. Once finished with that chore, she went into their bathroom and put their things together and tried to pack their toiletries in their respective suitcases.

She looked at Ginger's purse sitting on the chair next to the bed. Feeling a little guilty, she opened the purse and saw that their checkbook was in the bottom of the purse. She opened it and began looking at the entries and the checks that Ginger and Fred had written over the past few months. She noticed that there was a lot of money going out of their account and not much coming in except their social security checks. Their account showed a balance of four hundred dollars. She checked back a couple of months and noticed that they generally carried a balance of four to five thousand dollars.

I wonder what was going on? She thought. *It looks like they were running out of money.*

She continued to look at some of the other things in Ginger's purse. There was a credit card statement in one of the side pockets. The balance on the statement was fourteen thousand dollars and was a couple of weeks past due. A lot of the charges on the account were from grocery stores and service stations. There were no major purchases of any large appliances or large electronic equipment.

Ginger was charging everything. Fourteen thousand dollars on her credit card and four hundred dollars in her account. Maybe they had other accounts and money somewhere else, but why carry such a small balance? Maybe they were in trouble financially like the detective said, she wondered.

She closed the suitcases and put them on the bed. She took Ginger's purse and set it beside the suitcases. She noticed Fred's wallet sitting on top of the dresser. She picked it up and looked through it. Nothing except some cash and a few credit cards were in the wallet so she opened his suitcase and put the wallet inside and closed it.

Debbie was wide awake now and decided to go into Tom and Pam Decker's room and do the same thing. Tom and Pam's room was a little more organized so it didn't take her as long to get things packed. She knew that Pam had taken her purse with her so there was nothing to look at relative to papers. She was surprised, however, to find Pam and Tom's checkbook in Pam's suitcase.

She must have left it there by mistake as she was distraught and in a hurry when she left. I guess it would not hurt to take a peek, she thought.

Debbie picked up the checkbook and started to look through it. She was amazed at how many large checks were written to some casino in Reno. The checkbook showed large sums being transferred from some other account into the check book and then checks written to the casino in roughly the same amount.

Debbie quickly estimated the amount that was cashed in the casino and concluded it was over one hundred thousand dollars. *I wonder if Tom knew about this?* she thought. She closed the suitcases and walked out of the room. When she got to her room she found that George was already asleep.

I'll take an Advil PM and that should put me to sleep. I'll talk to George about what I found in the morning.

Even though Debbie took the pill to help her sleep, she lay there in bed a long time thinking about what she had discovered in Ginger's and Pam's rooms. As she listened to her husband's breathing, she concluded that there was no question in her mind that Fred and Ginger were having financial problems. She also believed that Pam had developed a bad gambling habit.

Maybe George is right, she thought. *Maybe the lottery ticket has something to do with these accidents. However, both the couples that may have had financial problems are dead. Could the detective be right about Dave and his involvement in Fred and Ginger's death? Could Dave and Norma also be having financial problems?*

She kept thinking about how she was going to approach George about her conclusions and finally fell asleep.

While Debbie was getting the rooms organized, Dave and Norma Wheeler were having a conversation about the day's happenings.

Norma started it off by saying, "Dave, did you have anything to do with Fred and Ginger today like the detective thinks?"

"No," he responded. *I'm not going to get into this with Norma. She'd freak out.* "As I told the detective, I had a flat tire and fixed it. That's why it took me so long."

"I hope you were not involved, because…"

"I told you Norma," Dave interrupted, "I was not involved. You need to believe me about this."

"The detective must think something else. Why was he questioning you so closely?"

"He has to do his duty and question me because I was the only one that left the dinner table."

Norma did not say anything for a few minutes as she was getting ready for bed.

"I think the lottery ticket is the answer to our problems," she continued. "We should have enough money to pay Jack what's-his-name, and still be OK, don't you?"

"I don't know what Jack Williams will do once he learns we hit the lottery. He may want a bunch more money."

"God I hope not. In any case I just hope you didn't do anything stupid here and think we could get more of the lottery share by eliminating some of our friends."

"Jesus Christ, Norma, how many times do I have to tell you that I had nothing to do with Fred and Ginger's deaths."

"I hope I can read a little before I try to go to sleep. This whole thing has really got me upset," she added.

Dave felt himself getting pissed. *I'm doing this for us so we can live a nice life, and she does not appreciate it. What the hell does she want me to do? I don't give a damn what she thinks, I'm going to carry through with my next move.*

CHAPTER 29

Detective Morrison was just about home when his cell phone rang.

Who in the hell is calling me at this hour, he thought. "Morrison," he answered.

"Detective Morrison, my name is Taylor Decker, the son of Tom and Pam Decker."

Be careful with this call, Detective Morrison thought. "Mr. Decker, I'm really sorry about your parents. That must be one hell of a thing to try and handle."

"Can you tell me exactly what happened to my father?" asked Taylor.

"The only thing I can tell you right now is that it appeared to be an accident. There were some things that made me suspicious, but nothing substantial."

"What kind of things?"

"We could not tell for sure if the golf cart fell on him and broke his neck, or if he was incapacitated prior to the roll-over."

"Who was with him at the time of the so-called accident?" Taylor wanted to know.

"His long time friend Fred Bellows."

"What does he say about what happened?"

"Well, Mr. Decker, it gets rather complicated. This evening both Mr. Bellows and his wife died. They were sitting in a Jacuzzi when the electric wine chiller they were using slipped into the water. They were both electrocuted."

There was a long moment of silence on the phone.

"We have basically stopped the investigation into your father's death because the only witness is no longer with us," Detective Morrison went on.

"What about my mother's accident? What have you heard about that?" Taylor wanted to know.

"I'm in contact with the California Highway Patrol. They are going to do a complete investigation in the morning. Right now it looks like she lost control of the car. At this point we don't know anything else."

Again there was a long silence on the phone.

"Mr. Decker, I suggest you try and get some sleep. We should know more about your mother's accident tomorrow. Once again I'm terribly sorry for what happened today. I'm doing the best I can to get to the bottom of it all."

The silence continued on Taylor's side of the phone.

"Mr. Decker, are you there?"

"Yes, I'm here. I just don't know what to think at this point."

"I've had a long day. I have your phone number now that you called. I'll contact you as soon as I know something. I'm going to hang up now, and I'll talk to you tomorrow," Detective Morrison said. He hit the exit button on his phone and went in his house.

Taylor Decker sat on the hotel bed for another five minutes thinking about the conversation he had with the detective.

I guess he's doing all that he can, he thought. *I'll wait until tomorrow to see what develops. I should try and get some rest.*

Taylor kept thinking about his parents and what their deaths meant to him and his family. He could feel his heart beating in his chest as he tried to relax. He lay there in the hotel bed for another hour. He finally drifted off thinking about his future without his parents.

CHAPTER 30

It was a beautiful morning in Russell Cove. The fog stayed off the coast, and the sun was bright and warm. Dave and Norma Wheeler were up early, and Norma was fixing coffee for everyone. Dave left to go down and purchase a morning newspaper. The other two couples were not awake yet, at least they had not appeared in the kitchen for their morning coffee.

George and Debbie Mitchell were up and getting dressed. Debbie had thought about how she was going to approach George on what she had found in Pam's and Ginger's rooms last night. She decided just to be honest and let him know what she found and what her thoughts were.

"George, last night when I was putting Fred and Ginger's things away, I looked in her purse and discovered a few things."

"You looked in her purse?" George asked.

"Yes. And what I found was that they didn't have much money in their checking account, and there was a large balance past due on their charge card."

"The detective said he thought that Fred was in some kind of real estate deal that went sour. If Fred was having money trouble maybe my guess was right. Maybe he did have something to do with Tom's death because he wanted a bigger part of the lottery money," George said.

"But what about the families? They would get the part from their parents, wouldn't they?" Debbie asked.

"The only way that would not happen is if there is only one couple to claim the money, or if the couples that were left told everyone that they were the only ones who participated in the lottery ticket."

"That would be terrible," Debbie mentioned. "I also found Pam's checkbook in her suitcase and she had large amounts of money transferred to her account, and a lot of large checks written to a casino in Reno."

"Really?" George asked.

"Yes, I thought about it last night and really think she had a gambling problem."

"Well, that's two couples that were having financial troubles," George said thoughtfully. "I wonder about Dave and Norma."

"Well, Jim doesn't think that Dave had anything to do with the death of Fred and Ginger. Remember he said that there was no way that Dave could have set things up that quickly."

George suddenly remembered hearing a garage door open yesterday afternoon while they were in their rooms relaxing before dinner. He wondered if what he heard was Dave Wheeler opening up the garage and putting his car in so he could take care of his tire.

"I think I have some questions for Dave this morning," said George.

They both walked out of their room and down to the kitchen where they joined Norma for a cup of coffee.

Jim and Linda Schroeder were also up and getting dressed in their room. Linda was much better relative to her emotional condition but did not feel that well. She almost didn't go down to the kitchen with Jim, but Jim insisted she join him as some food would do her good. They entered the kitchen just as Norma was explaining to George and Debbie that Dave was out getting the paper.

Norma Wheeler looked at Linda and was a little shocked, "Are you alright Linda?" Norma asked.

"I'll make it. A cup of coffee would do me good."

Dave Wheeler came back into the house. He had the morning paper with him and looked a little disturbed.

"I bought this paper in a grocery store. The first thing the clerk said to me was if I noticed that someone in Russell Cove won the lottery yesterday. He said it was worth twenty-one million dollars. He said the person who won has not come forth with the ticket yet," Dave said.

"How do they know that?" Debbie asked.

"The numbers are recorded at their headquarters when the ticket is purchased. They know where it was purchased but as you don't have to sign anything, they don't know who purchased it," Dave responded.

"I think the place that sold the ticket gets some percentage of the amount or a flat fee," George said.

Their conversation was interrupted by the sound of the phone ringing. "I'll get it," George said as he started to get up and move to the phone.

"Why don't you try to eat something," Jim Schroeder told his wife.

"I'll have some toast. That's all I want," Linda responded.

Jim went to get the toaster while Debbie and Norma picked at some of the muffins and Danish that they had put on a plate. George came back into the room and said, "That was Taylor Decker. He sounded really shook up. He has rented a car and is coming up here to pick up Tom and Pam's things. He told me that he has been in contact with the authorities and is having both his dad and mom's bodies moved to Phoenix. He said the items that were being kept for studying would be delivered to the rental house this morning. He figures it will be a couple of hours before he gets here."

"I guess we need to pack their things that are in their room," Norma said. "God what a terrible thing."

"I did that last night," responded Debbie. "I also put Fred and Ginger's things together."

"We'll have to figure what to do with Fred's car," said George.

"Do we have to talk about this?" said Linda Schroeder.

"It's a beautiful day," Jim Schroeder said. "We need to take a walk this morning. Once we are out in the fresh air we'll all feel better."

"I don't know if I can walk the whole way," responded his wife Linda.

"We'll take it nice and slow. You'll feel better once you get out in the fresh air," Jim said.

"Dave, I'm going to take the lottery ticket and claim it today," George Mitchell said rather forcefully.

"That's fine," Dave Wheeler responded. "I'll go with you, and we'll get the process started."

"Did the paper mention anything about any other winners on our ticket?" Norma Wheeler asked her husband.

"Nothing was mentioned specifically so I would assume that we are the only winners," Dave responded.

"Are you having any financial problems?" George Mitchell asked Dave Wheeler.

"What do you mean?" Dave responded.

"I mean what I asked. Are you having any financial problems?"

"First of all I resent your implication. Second, it's none of your business what my financial situation is. I don't need to tell you or anyone else about anything to do with my financial situation."

George and Dave sat on either side of the table and looked intently at each other.

George continued, "When we went to dinner last night, your car was in the garage. In the afternoon it was on the street. Why did you move it into the garage?"

"After Pam left and there was an empty space, I wanted my car in the garage. Is that a crime?" Dave responded.

"Jim's right," interrupted Debbie. "It's a beautiful day for a walk. I agree with Jim. I think it would do us all good to get out for awhile."

"I want to go home as soon as possible," Linda said. "I want to get away from this house and this area. What used to be happy memories have turned into a nightmare."

"All right. Let's go get our walking shoes on and take the walk," George said still looking at Dave.

"You all go ahead. For some reason I have a splitting headache. I don't feel like walking right now," said Dave. "I may go back to my room and take a couple of aspirin and lie down for awhile."

"Do you want me to stay with you?" asked Norma.

"No, I'll be fine in a little while. You go ahead," answered Dave.

The group went upstairs to their rooms to get ready for the walk. When they returned, Dave Wheeler was still sitting at the kitchen table reading the newspaper.

"We're going to take it nice and easy," Jim relayed. "We're going to the left as I don't want to challenge the steep hill."

Jim was remembering that you go up a gradual incline and down a steep hill if you go in the direction he mentioned.

"We'll all take it nice and easy," responded Debbie. "I don't think any of us got much sleep last night."

LAST WALK AT RUSSELL COVE

"I really don't want to do this," Linda Schroeder relayed. "In fact, I'm not coming back to this area again; there are too many bad memories."

"You may change your mind in a few months," said Norma Wheeler. "Time does a lot to heal bad memories."

"No, I'm not going to change my mind," Linda said rather strongly. "This is going to be my last walk at Russell Cove."

CHAPTER 31

Detective Wilt Morrison was up early that morning even thought he didn't get to bed until after midnight. He was having his morning coffee while reading the newspaper. He was skimming the stories as his mind was still on the four people who had died the day before. He noticed that someone had won twenty-one million dollars in the lottery in Russell Cove. He thought how lucky that individual was, as you can do a lot with all that money.

Pearl joined him for a cup of coffee. When he came home from the Jacuzzi episode, he found her waiting up for him. He told her what he had found and some of the things he was thinking about. She now believed that the motive was money as the love angle didn't seem to fit anymore.

He finished his coffee and put a call into the video store where last night Dave Wheeler turned in the video of *The Birds*. He was hoping to find a few more late videos or DVD's turned in so he could verify Mr. Wheeler's alibi or prove he didn't change a tire in that parking lot.

He was disappointed to learn that there was only one video turned in last night. It was rented by a Dr. Schroeder he was told. That meant Detective Morrison didn't have any leads to go on or any person to interview. Now, he would have to try and canvas the area to see if anyone noticed a man changing his tire in the parking lot. He told Pearl about his problem.

"Maybe someone saw him drive up to the house. What kind of car does he drive?" she asked.

"He drives some kind of BMW. Great idea, Pearl, I should have thought of that. I'll get someone to canvas the area. That is much easier than going from house to house in Russell Cove."

"You may have to do both," she said.

Detective Morrison called the San Francisco headquarters of the California Highway Patrol. After explaining who he was to a few officers, he reached the individual in charge of investigating accidents. He asked the individual if they had had enough time to determine the cause of the accident yesterday afternoon that happened just before the tunnel leading to the Golden Gate Bridge. The individual put him on hold for a moment and came back and told him that so far it looked like a simple case of the driver losing control of her car. Detective Morrison asked if they had done a thorough inspection of the car. He was told that time had not allowed that but it would be done sometime today.

"I would appreciate it if you could make it a priority," Detective Morrison said. "I suspect some foul play. I have reason to believe someone may have done something to cause a mechanical problem."

He was assured they would get right on the inspection. The individual took his phone number and told him he would call him back after they had finished.

Detective Morrison called a friend of his who was an electrician. He explained what happened last night. He asked if it was possible that the main circuit breaker would stay closed long enough to kill the two people in the Jacuzzi. His friend told him that it was possible but unusual as the breaker would open within a quarter or sixteenth of a second after the wine chiller was thrown into the water.

"It really depends on a lot of things. First if the circuit breaker was working properly. Second what kind of shape the people were in physically. They may have received one hell of a shock, but could probably have survived. Maybe the wiring in the house is not up to code."

"What would it take to force the main breaker to remain closed?"

"The most common way is to shove something like a screwdriver behind the breaker so it could not move. Did you take a good look at the breaker to see if there were any scratch marks around it?"

"Yes, and I didn't see any marks that would indicate some one played around with it."

"All you would have to do is put tape around the screwdriver and that would prevent any scratch marks," his friend said.

Shit, thought Detective Morrison. *Dave Wheeler had a*

screwdriver in his trunk with tape around the blade. I need to take a closer look at that tool.

He thanked his friend for the information and hung up the phone.

He looked at his notes and remembered he had asked all of them for their home address. He selected the loose sheet of paper with Dave and Norma Wheeler's address on it. He called the sheriff's office in Glendale, California. He explained what he wanted and asked if he could wait while they looked up Dave Wheeler's name to see if he had ever been in any kind of trouble. After a few minutes he was told that there was no Dave Wheeler in their data banks, which meant he was clean as far as they were concerned.

Detective Morrison called the Medical Examiner and was told Dr. Larry Gravits was not at work yet. He asked his assistant if any fingerprints were taken off the extension cord yet. After a minute the assistant told him there were several prints on the cord, but none matched either of the diseased. Detective Morrison thanked the assistant and hung up the phone.

It's starting to come together, he thought. *I think that Dave Wheeler came back to the house from dropping off the tape, jammed the circuit breaker, got the extension cord and the wine chiller and dropped it in the Jacuzzi. He then put the screwdriver in his trunk with the flat tire, which he had done himself earlier. He probably even scraped the jack in the dirt so it looked like it had been used. But why? What did he have to gain?*

As he was sitting there, he remembered he had to call Tammy Riley, daughter of Fred and Ginger Bellows. He found the slip of paper that Debbie Mitchell had given him last night and made the call.

As expected, Linda Riley was devastated to learn the news about her parents. Her husband, Bob Riley, who was working at home that morning, had to take over the phone when his wife could no longer continue the conversation. Bob Riley asked questions about the deaths and at the same time tried to calm his wife. He took Detective Morrison's phone number and said they would call back as soon as they had a chance to discuss the situation and make some plans. Detective Morrison gave them the phone number and address of the rental house. He expressed his sorrow once again and ended the conversation.

Feeling somewhat depressed after the phone call, Detective Morrison finished his breakfast, kissed Pearl, got in his car, and started for his office. He decided to call the DA's office and speak to one of the lawyers there about the situation. He wanted their advice to determine if he had enough information to bring Dave Wheeler in for questioning. As he thought about it, he really didn't have much that a good defense lawyer couldn't explain away. He could hear the defense in his mind.

The couple in the Jacuzzi were distraught from the death of their friends. Because of their distress, they were careless about the wine chiller. There are too many fingerprints on the extension cord to draw any conclusions. The radio could have been affected by the electricity going off. Just because no one saw Mr. Wheeler in the parking lot doesn't mean he wasn't there. There are no witnesses that saw his car near the house prior to the wine chiller falling in the Jacuzzi. Most of us have tape around our screwdrivers to prevent scratches for what ever we are doing. He did have a flat tire in his trunk, and was dirty when he came back to join his friends for dinner. Any one of these situations could mean a reasonable doubt that he was involved in the death of Mr. and Mrs. Bellows.

The ringing of his cell phone brought him out of his thought pattern.

"Morrison," he answered.

"Detective Morrison, it's William Anderson again, the paramedic out here at Russell Cove. We were called back to the rental house this morning. You know, the house where the five couples are staying. You're not going to believe what I have to tell you."

CHAPTER 32

The five individuals left the rental house and started on their walk. George and Debbie Mitchell, along with Norma Wheeler, lagged behind. They let Jim and Linda Schroeder go ahead of them. They knew that Linda was distraught, and thought it best that she and her husband walk by themselves.

Jim Schroeder was concerned about his wife and her condition. He started talking to her in a quiet voice. "Linda, you have to gather your strength and be strong through all of this. I know it's a terrible thing to lose good friends. Since we only see them once a year, you can pretend that they are still alive, and you just can't see them anymore."

Linda kept walking alongside her husband, looking forward, and not saying anything.

Jim continued, "Let's see if we can gain something positive about these accidents. Knowing them, they would want us to continue on with our lives. They would want us to try to be happy. Just think, their families will have money now and that's a good thing. It's a beautiful day. Look around at the scenery and how pretty everything is."

"What about our lives?" she said, finally breaking her silence. "We're facing a major financial problem, and I don't know how that's going to turn out."

"Well, maybe if we explain our situation to George and Dave, they will let us borrow some of their winnings until we can get through our situation. I can always go back to work and keep money coming in through my practice."

"If you still have a practice after all this is over."

"I'll pay off the two blackmailers. We still have the equity in our house. With that and what we can borrow, we'll be OK," Jim said trying to give his wife some encouragement.

"No we will not," she replied. "I don't want to discuss it any more now, let's just go back to the house, pack our things, and go home."

"Let's finish the walk, and then we'll leave just as soon as we can."

George and Debbie Mitchell were walking with Norma Wheeler. George wanted to talk about his concerns relative to the accidents but hesitated to bring up the subject. He was afraid that Norma would get upset. She was the one who started the conversation.

"This whole thing is terrible," Norma said. "I talked to Dave about what he was doing last night. I'm convinced that he feels as bad about what has happened as we all do."

"You're probably right Norma," George chimed in. "I guess I got carried away asking him questions, but I was thinking about what the detective said and his concerns about how the accident happened."

"Financially we're doing fine," Norma lied. "Dave received several nice bonuses from his company that put us in a good position for retirement."

"That's nice," George Mitchell responded. "It's just that we suspect that Tom and Pam, as well as Fred and Ginger were having some money problems. They all could have wanted more of their share of the lottery winnings."

"How do you know that?" Norma asked.

"When I was getting their items packed, I noticed some things that lead me to believe they were in trouble," Debbie added.

"What did you do, go through some of their personal items?" Norma asked.

"It doesn't matter how she found out," George said. "It is still hard for me to believe that the lottery money doesn't have something to do with what is going on."

"Well, it certainly is nothing we have done," added Norma. "We've been friends now for over forty years. I just can't imagine why any one of us would want anything bad to happen to any of us."

"I couldn't agree more," George Mitchell said. *But I'm really not convinced that is the case.*

As they continued their walk, they didn't know that a BMW was backing out of the rental house garage.

CHAPTER 33

Dave Wheeler sat at the table in the kitchen. He watched the five individuals leave for their walk. He thought about what he was going to do, and what effect it would have on him, his wife and his retirement.

I told them I have a terrible headache, he thought. *I was going to town to get gas. So, I blacked out or don't remember what happened. That's a good excuse, and maybe they will believe it. Even if they don't, and charge me with manslaughter, with my record they probably will not give me more that a couple of years. Even if I get five or six years I can get out in two or three. After that it will be clear sailing from then on.*

He sat at the table and thought some more. *With the money from the lottery, if that asshole Jack Williams wants more money I can hire someone to get rid of him. Plus, this would take the attention off the suspicion of me being involved in the deaths of Fred and Ginger.*

He got up from the table, went out, and got in his car. He sat there for a few more minutes trying to get his courage to the point of carrying out his plan. He started his car, backed out of the garage and started up the incline toward the steep downhill grade. Based on the time they left, he figured the five people would be walking down the steep hill about now. He drove to the top of the hill and stopped. Half way down the hill he saw all of them walking. Norma was walking to the left of Debbie and George Mitchell. About twenty yards in front of them were Jim and Linda. The road was two lanes, and to the right was a fairly steep drop off into the brush. On the left of where Dave was sitting was a ten-foot high dirt bank. On top of the bank were some houses. Dave figured he could hit Debbie and George without hitting Norma, and then hit Jim and Linda. He knew he needed some speed to ensure all four of them would be hit so hard that it would kill them. He took a deep breath and started down the hill. He wanted to proceed with a speed of around forty miles per hour so he put his foot down on the accelerator.

Norma, Debbie and George were walking at a fairly slow pace down the hill. Norma was on the inside toward the dirt bank walking next to Debbie, with George on the outside next to the drop off. The two ladies were carrying on a conversation about the events of yesterday when Norma noticed out of the corner of her eye a car approaching at a fast speed down the hill. The car was over next to the drop off and heading straight for Debbie and George. Norma didn't have time to see who was driving but knew Debbie and George were in danger of being hit. She acted quickly and shoved Debbie hard toward the drop off. Debbie hit George and both of them stumbled and went over the side of the road. This action put Norma directly in front of the oncoming car, and it hit her throwing her directly in the car's windshield. She was hit with such force that her head went half way through the windshield, killing her instantly. Her eyes were still open as she died, looking at the driver of the car.

Dave was shocked to see his wife Norma push Debbie and George out of the way of his car. In that instant he didn't think of the consequences of his wife's action until he heard the thud as Norma hit the windshield. When Dave focused on the object in front of him he could see her face through the cracked windshield. He froze as she stared at him with her dead eyes open. His mind went blank as he felt the ground go out from underneath the car as it left the road. He kept staring at his wife as the car started to tip upside down. His last emotion was a sick, empty feeling as the car landed on its top, skidding forward in the dirt, smashing the whole top of the car, and pushing Norma clear through the windshield into her husband. The car rolled onto its side and came to rest about forty feet down the bank from the road. As it finally came to a stop, it rolled once more and stopped right side up, with dust and broken brush limbs flying in the air.

At first George and Debbie didn't know what was happening. They knew that Norma was pushing them sideways, and they knew they were going to fall off the road down the bank. Both of them tried to twist so their bodies would fall forward. They both stopped themselves about five feet down the bank by putting their heels in the dirt and sitting down. About the time they stopped sliding they heard the noise of the car hitting the dirt and rolling over.

"Holy shit!" George exclaimed. He looked at his wife and said, "Are you all right?"

"I'm scraped up a little, but I'm OK," Debbie responded.

They both climbed back up to the road and started down the road where the car left the pavement. Jim and Linda were already coming up the hill and met them at the accident spot.

"I didn't see what happened," Jim said.

"I think Dave tired to run over us!" exclaimed George. "Norma pushed us out of the way and stepped in front of the car, which hit her."

"Let's go down to the car and see what we can do. Debbie, please call 911 and tell them what happened and that we may have some real injuries on our hand," said Jim.

Debbie was starting to pull out her phone when George and Jim started down the bank towards the car. She tried to get the phone to work, but received no signal. She ran over to Linda and asked her for her phone. At first Linda just stood their looking at the wrecked car.

"Linda," Debbie said. "Give me your cell phone!"

Linda slowly looked at Debbie, reached in her pocket, and handed Debbie the phone. Debbie called 911.

When George arrived at the overturned car, they saw how Norma had been pushed through the windshield and was certainly dead. They looked at Dave and decided that he was also dead as the top of the car had crushed him when it landed upside down.

"Let's see if we can get Dave out of the car," said Jim.

"I don't think it will do any good, Jim. I think he's already gone."

"The car may catch on fire and explode," Jim responded.

"There's no smoke anywhere. I don't think that's going to happen."

"Come on," Jim insisted. "Help me get the car door open."

Jim started pulling on the door of the driver's side. Even though it had been smashed from the top, the door started to open slightly with Jim's efforts. George stood there for a minute and watched as Jim struggled with the door. He went over and started helping Jim muscle the door open. After some effort the door started to open which gave the two men more leverage. After five minutes of pushing and pulling the door was open enough to get Dave out of the car. The air bag had inflated, but it had not helped Dave's situation as his head was crushed from the car's roof. Although Norma was wedged in on top of Dave, Jim and George managed to free Dave's body and pull him out of the car. They dragged Dave's body about ten feet from the car and both stood there sweating and breathing hard. George looked at Jim, who was pale and breathing heavy.

"Are you all right?" George asked Jim.

"I'm fine," Jim responded as he bent down and rolled Dave over on his stomach.

"What are you doing?" George wanted to know.

Jim didn't say anything but reached into Dave's back pocket and pulled out his wallet.

"No sense letting the lottery ticket go with the body," Jim said as he pulled the ticket out of the wallet.

"How the hell can you think of the lottery ticket at a time like this?" George demanded.

"Look George, this ticket is worth a lot of money, and it's not going to do Dave and Norma any good now. In fact as there are only two of us left, that's a bunch of money each."

"What the hell are you talking about? Even though our other friends have died, we should split the money with their families."

"Their families don't need to know that they participated. We can say that it was just the two of us who bought the ticket and split the money. That's over ten million each before taxes and shit. I need the money and I'm sure you could use it too."

"That's bullshit, Jim." George could not believe they were having this conversation with their friend lying dead at their feet.

"George, just think about it, OK," Jim said, still breathing hard.

They could hear the ambulance and the fire truck coming up the road in the distance.

"Don't do something now that you will regret later," Jim continued. "Let's keep the ticket under raps until we have a chance to discuss this at a better time. Right now what we have to concentrate on is letting the authorities know what happened here and how Dave and Norma died."

"What are you two doing down there?" Debbie yelled from the road. She had witnessed Jim turning over Dave's body and doing something with his wallet. "Are they both gone?" She could not bring herself to say the word dead.

Jim started climbing back up to the road, and George followed. When they reached the road George told Debbie and Linda that both Dave and Norma had died in the accident. He wrapped his arms around Debbie as she started sobbing in his shoulder. Linda just stood there looking at Jim and said nothing. She didn't express any emotion at all, like she was in some kind of trance.

"I better get you back to the house as soon as we can," Jim said to Linda.

The two vehicles arrived, and it didn't take long for the paramedics to analyze the situation and slide down the hill to where the car was resting. They noticed Dave's body lying about ten feet from the car. They also noticed Norma's body wedged in the front seat with her feet still protruding from the windshield. They quickly examined both bodies and determined very quickly that both were deceased. They also noticed that the driver's door was open and yelled up to the four people standing on the road.

"How did he get thrown from the car?" one of the paramedics asked.

Both George and Jim went back down the hill to where the paramedics were standing.

"I'm a doctor," Jim said. "I was not sure Dave's injury was fatal and wanted to get him away from the car in case there was any fire. Mr. Mitchell and I got the car door opened and pulled out Dave's body. It was not until we pulled him out that I was sure he was gone."

The paramedic looked at Dr. Schroeder with somewhat of a puzzled look as he thought to himself that it should have been obvious that the man had been killed in the accident.

"Did you two witness this accident?" the paramedic asked.

"Yes," responded George. We were all walking down the road when Dave's car came up behind us. He hit his wife Norma and then ran off the road. You can see the result."

"As this has been a fatal accident, I have to call the Sheriff's office to report it. Please stay around until a detective gets here as I'm sure he will have some questions."

"I'm worried about my wife," Jim responded. "I think she is at the end of her emotions, and I really want to get her back to the house so she can get a sedative and some rest. All this had been very hard on her."

"That's fine, Doctor," the paramedic said. "I'm sure the individual from the sheriff's office can find you as we all know where you are staying."

With that response, Jim started back up the hill toward the two ladies, who were standing on the road with two men who came with the fire engine. When Jim got to the top of the hill, he took Linda by the arm.

"Come on Linda. I need to take you back to the house so you can get some rest."

"You don't look very good either," Debbie said. "Are you going to be all right?"

"I'll be fine. I'm worried about Linda right now. She may be going into emotional shock and needs to get a sedative and some rest. We'll see you back at the house."

Debbie watched both of them as they started up the hill. She turned to one of the firemen standing on the road.

"Could you give a ride to those two?" she asked, pointing to Jim and Linda who were walking up the hill.

"Sorry ma'am," he responded. "We need to stay here until we are sure the car will not catch on fire. You never know when this fire engine is going to be needed."

George came back up the hill and stood by Debbie.

"What was Jim doing down there?" she asked. "It looked like he pulled something out of Dave's pants."

"He wanted to get the lottery ticket," George said looking somewhat disgusted.

"You're kidding."

"No, I'm not kidding. Not only that but he wants us to say that the only two couples who participated in the ticket were the Schroeder's and us. That way we would not have to split the money with anyone except the four of us."

"What about the families of our friends who were killed?"

"Jim said he needs the money, and three or four million after taxes is much better than a little over one million."

"I will not do that," Debbie said rather firmly.

"He does not want us to make a decision on that now. He wants us to talk about it once things settle down."

"That's just not right," Debbie continued.

"I know, I know."

"The families deserve the money just as much as we do," she continued.

"Look Debbie, I said I agree with you. I just told you what Jim said and that we wants to discuss it later, when things settle down."

Debbie changed the subject. "George, do you think Dave was trying to hit us when Norma pushed us out of the way?"

"Well, it sure looks that way. If she had not shoved us, we would have been hit for sure."

"Why do you think Dave would want to kill us?" she asked.

"I don't know what to think. I'm sure we would have been hit. Maybe Dave lost control or passed out or something. I know we had an argument this morning, but I didn't think he was mad enough to try and kill me. If he was, why was he trying to hit both of us?" George responded.

"I don't think he was that upset either. I don't know about any health problems. Not only that, but he was going to lie down when we left. What was he doing driving his car and going in our direction?"

"That's a good question Debbie."

"He said he had a terrible headache. I wonder if that had anything to do with this?"

"I don't know. At this point I don't think we'll ever know," George responded.

"Are you going to tell the detective about the lottery ticket?"

George thought a moment. "I don't know what I'm going to do about that either."

George looked down the road as a sheriff's car pulled up. An individual got out of the car and started walking toward them.

"Shit," George mumbled. "It's the same detective that we've had all along. I guess we're going to have to answer his questions as best as we can."

"I think we should tell him," said Debbie.

"I don't know; let's wait until we talk to Jim."

Debbie looked at her husband and determined that she was not going to wait.

CHAPTER 34

Jim and Linda Schroeder continued up the hill walking back to the rental house. Although they were only half way down before turning around after the accident, the hill seemed longer and steeper than either of them anticipated. Jim felt himself getting more tired by the minute. He tried not to think of himself as he was concerned about his wife and how she was taking the loss of all her friends. He tried to carry on a conversation, at the same time trying to maintain his breath while walking.

"That was really too bad," he said to Linda. "I don't really know what happened. Maybe Dave passed out or something because he told us he had a headache. Don't you remember?"

Linda looked at her husband with a blank expression.

"Don't you remember Dave talking about a headache?" he asked again.

"Yes," she responded.

"What do you think? Do you think he may have had a health problem and passed out?"

"I don't know what to think. All this terrible death is too much for me to think about."

Jim kept on talking as they reached the crest of the hill and started the slight incline down to the house. He was still breathing heavily and was having a hard time getting his lungs full of air. He also noticed a slight pulsating pain in his left side. He tried to ignore it and concentrate on Linda and how she was doing.

When they reached the house he took her upstairs to the bedroom and suddenly felt the urge to lie down. He knew he had to give the sedative to Linda so he walked into the bathroom, found the pills behind the mirror, got a glass of water and handed it to her. She looked at it, then put the pill in her mouth and swallowed it with the water.

"I have to lie down," he said. "For some reason that walk really tired me out. Let me lie here and get my breath. You can also lie down with me and get some rest. We'll both feel better in a little while."

For the first time since the car accident, Linda looked and actually studied her husband. She noticed he was pale and still sweating a little from the walk up the hill. She gathered her strength and told herself that her husband needed her so she should be strong. She thought she should also lie down beside Jim and rest for a few minutes as she felt the pill start to relax her. As she fell asleep, she didn't notice that her husband, who was lying beside her, was no longer breathing.

CHAPTER 35

Detective Morrison was in his car and on the way to the accident. He thought the paramedic was right, as he could not believe what the paramedic told him.

Dave Wheeler hit his wife with his car and ran off the road, killing both of them? he thought.

He learned that the two couples that were staying at the house decided to take a walk, along with Dave Wheeler's wife Norma. Apparently Dave Wheeler drove his car into the group, hitting his wife. The other two couples were OK, but both Dave and his wife were killed. According to the paramedic, after Dave Wheeler hit his wife, his car continued straight rather than making a slight turn, following the road. As the car left the road it did a half turn in mid-air and came down on its top.

Detective Morrison was convinced that what had happened with the couples in that rental house in the last day and a half was no coincidence. Something was going on and there was something that someone was not telling him. He still thought that Tom Decker's death was a homicide, but it was a moot point as his suspected killer was dead. He also was convinced that Dave Wheeler was responsible for the deaths of Fred and Ginger Bellows. He thought he had enough evidence to put that together and now they were dead.

Why are these good friends killing each other? he thought as he headed for the accident site. *They come up here for fifteen years or more and all of a sudden they decide to commit murder. What the hell is going on?*

He tried to review the situations in his mind. The death on the golf course. How Fred Bellows had acted when questioned. The radio not playing by the Jacuzzi . How Dave Wheeler had acted about the death of Fred and Ginger. He decided that the two couples who were left had alibis and were probably not involved in any of the so-called accidents.

George Mitchell had his number in Mrs. Decker's cell phone like he was expecting something was going to happen to her and wanted to know when.

He thought about the car that Pam Decker was driving. He pulled out his cell phone and called the individual who he had contacted before to ask about the investigation. He learned that it looked like the brake fluid on Pan Decker's car was very low, and the warning lights were removed. There was no doubt in the inspector's mind that someone had tampered with her car, causing it to lose its brakes and go out of control. He told Detective Morrison that he would contact him in the next day or two to discuss possible suspects. Detective Morrison thanked him and hung up the phone.

He continued to explore the different possibilities in his mind. He wondered if Fred Bellows and George Mitchell might be in this together?

Someone had to have the time and knowledge to screw with the car. Who was at the house alone yesterday morning? Fred Bellows went back to the house after the golf cart accident and spent at least an hour alone. He could have taken out the brake fluid and the fuses then. Why would he want to kill them both? Couples! Tom and Pam were a couple. Fred and Ginger were a couple. Now Dave and Norma, all were couples.

It seemed to Detective Morrison that if someone were mad or vindictive they would get back at an individual, not the individual and his or her spouse. He could understand if someone wanted to kill Fred or Ginger, they just happened to both be together in the Jacuzzi. But Tom and Pam? Someone wanted to get rid of both of them. Logically it followed that someone wanted to get rid of both Fred and Ginger also. But it was different people doing the killing.

Maybe they are playing some kind of Dungeons and Dragons game or something where all try and kill each other, and the winner gets the stash of money, he thought.

He recalled the phone conversation he had with Taylor Decker the night before. He wondered how much he should tell him about the cause of the accident. He didn't want anyone else asking questions and getting upset before he could get some answers.

His mind kept racing as he turned into the housing complex and started up the hill toward the accident.

I have to get to the bottom of this as there is something here that they are not telling me. I have to get more demanding until one of the couples left tells me what is going on, he thought.

As he parked his car, he saw George and Debbie Mitchell standing alongside the fire truck and the ambulance. He didn't see Jim and Linda Schroeder and wondered where they were. He got out and started toward George and Debbie, at the same time looking down the slope at the wrecked car and the body lying alongside.

CHAPTER 36

Detective Morrison walked up and stood next to Debbie and George Mitchell. No one said anything as he looked over the scene. After a few minutes he turned to Debbie and George and asked,

"Did you see the accident?"

"Yes," responded George. "We were walking along the road. Debbie, me and Dave's wife, Norma, were in one group, and Jim and Linda Schroeder were about twenty yards in front of us."

"We didn't hear the car coming," said Debbie. "Norma pushed us out of the way just before the car hit us. As she did that, it put her in front of the car. It hit her real hard."

"Do you think that Dave Wheeler was trying to hit and kill you?" asked Detective Morrison

"I don't know what to think," answered George. "The only thing I can tell you is that if Norma had not pushed us out of the way, we would have been hit for sure."

"Do you know of any reason that Mr. Wheeler wanted to kill you?"

"Well, we had an argument this morning, but I don't think he was upset enough to try and run me over," said George.

"What was the argument about?"

"I asked him about his financial situation, and he got pissed off at me."

"Why were you talking about that?" Detective Morrison asked.

George ignored the question. "He said he had a headache this morning so maybe he blacked out or had some kind of health problem. I don't know why he would want to run us down."

"It's the lottery ticket!" Debbie blurted out.

George rolled his eyes as Detective Morrison turned his attention toward Debbie.

"What lottery ticket?" Detective Morrison questioned.

Debbie looked at her husband. "I can't help it George. It's time the detective knew what we think is going on here." She turned to Detective Morrison and continued. "We all chipped in and bought a lottery ticket day before yesterday. We always do that when we come up here. We hit the jackpot yesterday and won twenty-one million dollars."

"I saw that in the paper. So that was your group that had the winning number?"

"Yes," Debbie said. "As it turns out we think Fred, Ginger and Tom and Pam were having financial difficulties. I think they were trying to kill some of us so they could get more of the winning money."

Detective Morrison thought for a moment. "That explains a lot. It puts some of the pieces of the puzzle together. Do you think that also applied to Dave Wheeler and his wife?"

"I don't know," chimed in George as he resigned himself to the fact that the detective now knew about the ticket. "We don't know of any problems they were having, but he did get real upset when I asked him the questions about it."

"I need to find out more about this situation," Detective Morrison said. "Right now I need to go down to the accident site and take a look. It is obvious that both of the individuals are dead. Was Dave Wheeler thrown out from the crash? Is that why his body is outside the car?"

"No," George said. "Dr. Schroeder wanted to pull him out because he thought he might still be alive and was concerned that the car might catch on fire and explode."

"Stop it George," Debbie said. "Let's start telling the truth about all this. I'm tired of trying to cover for people." She turned to Detective Morrison. "Jim pulled Dave's body out of the car because Dave had the lottery ticket in his pocket. He wanted to make sure it didn't leave the area."

Detective Morrison turned to George and asked, "Is that correct?"

"Yes, that's what happened," George said sheepishly.

"Where is Dr. Schroeder?" Detective Morrison asked.

"He wanted to get his wife back to the house as he thought she was going into some kind of shock," George responded. "He wanted to give her a sedative and get her to relax. She's not taking all of this very well. In fact would you mind if Debbie and I went back to the house also? We've been here for awhile and we'd like to leave."

"I'll take a look at the area and then come on over to the house. I need to get some information from both you and Dr. Schroeder and get this all wrapped up."

Debbie and George started walking back up the hill. Detective Morrison could not think of any way either one of them could be involved in any killing of their friends. They both had good alibis during the murders and were now being truthful with him. He also thought of Dr. Schroeder and came to the same conclusion relative to his whereabouts when the killings occurred. He was also convinced now that when the background check was done on each of the six individuals who had been killed, one would find some kind of financial problems.

He felt better about all of this as he walked down to the car. He took some pictures and looked around for about ten minutes. He thought about how the accident happened and how both individuals were killed. He walked back up to the road and took more pictures of where the car went off the bank. He walked to the top of the hill and took more pictures. He concluded that he was about finished. He had all the pictures he needed. Now he needed the statements from the two couples who witnessed the accident. Once that was done, he could complete the paper work and this whole mysterious case could be wrapped up.

He told the paramedics that he was finished, and they could move the bodies to the morgue. He knew they would also call a tow truck and get the area cleaned up. He took one last look and headed for his car.

CHAPTER 37

As George and Debbie were walking toward their rental house, George was thinking about the conversation he had with Jim while they were down at the car. He remembered Jim saying, "I need the money, and I'm sure you could use it too." He wondered if he needed it badly enough to kill someone for it. Now that there were only two couples left, were he and Debbie in danger?

"I think we may have to be a little careful," George said. "Jim is going to be real disappointed that we told the detective about the lottery ticket. I don't know what he may do."

"Well, it won't matter," Debbie added. "The detective now knows about the ticket. Jim's just going to have to accept that."

"He acted pretty desperate down at the car. He was going to get that ticket come hell or high water. He really started sweating and was not looking very good."

"If you recall he had a heart attack a couple of years ago. All this stress plus the physical exertion probably didn't do him any good."

"Well, we'll see when we get to the house."

Changing the subject, Debbie said, "I want to leave the house today as soon as we can. I want to get home."

"I don't have any problem with that. We probably should see if there is anything we can do for Dave and Norma's family. Or the other families for that matter. Someone has to take care of their things, and there is still Fred and Ginger's car and other stuff."

"The families will have enough money to get all that stuff done when they learn about the lottery ticket."

They walked for a little while without saying anything. George was thinking about the lottery ticket and how nice it would be to have more of the winnings. He was trying to think of some kind of compromise that Debbie would accept if he and Jim split the money half and half.

I guess it really doesn't matter now. The detective knows about all of us buying in, and we can't ask him to keep quiet about that, he thought.

George and Debbie entered the house and looked for Jim. George really didn't want to tell Jim about the conversation with Detective Morrison but he didn't have much choice. He also needed to let Jim know that the detective was coming over to the house to question them about what they saw. George and Debbie sat down in the living room and decided that Jim and Linda were in their rooms probably resting. George decided to go up to their room and alert Jim about the coming visit and also about the conversation. He walked to their room and lightly tapped on their door. He received no response. He opened the door and saw both of them lying on the bed. Linda was breathing deeply but Jim didn't seem to be moving. George quietly whispered Jim's name as he didn't want to wake Linda, knowing her condition. He received no response from Jim. George quietly moved into the room and went over to Jim. He saw that he was very pale and didn't seem to be breathing. George stood there for a moment as he didn't quite know what to do. He felt his heart increase its rhythm as he moved closer. Taking a deep breath he put his fingers on Jim's neck to see if he could feel a pulse. He felt nothing, and Jim felt cold. He gave Jim a little shake, but Jim didn't move.

Damn, I think he's dead, George thought. He backed out of the room and went back to where Debbie was in the living room.

"Debbie, we have a problem upstairs," George said taking a deep breath. As Debbie looked up, George continued. "Linda is sleeping soundly, but I can't wake Jim. I couldn't feel any pulse, and he's not breathing. I think he's dead."

"Oh God, George. What do you think happened?"

"Probably a heart attack. The stress was just too much for him, I guess."

"So, what do we do now?" Debbie asked.

George didn't say anything for a moment and told Debbie he would be right back. He went back up to Jim and Linda's room. He quietly walked in and went back over to Jim. Very slowly he reached under Jim's body until he could feel his wallet. He pulled it out, took out the lottery ticket, and then very carefully put the wallet back in the pocket. He left the room and went back downstairs.

"What did you do?" asked Debbie.

"I got the lottery ticket."

"The damn lottery ticket. I wish we'd never won the damn money."

"Listen Debbie, if we can talk to the detective, and if he'd not say anything about us telling him that we all participated in the cost of the ticket, I have an idea that you may agree to."

George proceeded to tell Debbie his idea. After discussing it back and fourth for a few minutes, Debbie finally relented.

"I guess I can live with that," Debbie said. "But I don't know if Linda will go along with it. And I think that Detective Morrison will never go along with the idea of not telling anyone about how all of us bought the ticket. It explains why so many people were killed. I think he just will not accept the fact that we want him to keep quiet."

"Well, it doesn't hurt to ask. The last thing I would do is bribe the detective. I think he's the kind of individual who would really take offense to that kind of idea."

"Well, I guess we'll find out as I see him coming up to the door."

CHAPTER 38

Detective Morrison was about to knock on the door when George opened it. He told the detective to come on into the living room as they needed to discuss something. Detective Morrison did what he as asked to do, but was looking around, apparently for Dr. Schroeder.

"Where is Dr. Schroeder?" he asked.

"We'll get to that in a moment, sir," George responded. "Before we get Jim, I'd like to ask you a favor."

"What's that?"

"Well, my wife and I have decided that we'd like to split the lottery ticket with only two couples, that being Linda, uh, Jim and Linda and ourselves. The only way we can do that is for you to forget that we told you we all participated in buying the ticket."

"I can't do that. Knowing about the lottery ticket will complete my report on all that happened here in the last couple of days," Detective Morrison said.

George continued, "Look detective, the suspected killer of Tom and Pam Decker, Fred Bellows is dead. Also the suspected killer of Fred and Ginger Bellows is also dead. What difference does it make now if those deaths go down as accidents, or known homicides with unknown motives? It will not matter to those who are dead."

"What about the families of the victims? Don't they deserve some of the money from the lottery?"

"Let us worry about the families. All we are asking is that you don't disclose the fact that all of us bought into the ticket."

"Sorry Mr. Mitchell, I can't do that. It is against my principles and ethics. I'm a detective. I have a job to do, and I'm going to do my job."

"Well, that's your choice. I guess you have to do what you think is best, but I still don't understand why."

"I thought for awhile there that you were going to try and bribe me with some of the lottery money. That would have been a huge mistake on your part."

"My wife and I don't think you are the bribing type. We would never think of doing that."

"Now, let's get back to the accident and the questions I may have. Would you mind going up and asking Dr. Schroeder to join us please?"

"Dr. Schroeder cannot join us," George said

"Why not?" asked Detective Morrison.

"Because he's dead. Apparently he had what looks like a heart attack and died in the bed as he was lying next to his wife. I checked on him when we came into the house and found him cold and not breathing. He's had heart problems before. I think the stress of his wife being unstable and the physical effort trying to get the wrecked car door open pushed his heart beyond the limit."

Detective Morrison stood there for a moment without saying anything. *I just don't fucking believe this,* he thought. *Another dead man on my hands.*

"Did you move him or touch anything?" the detective asked.

"Yes, I took out his wallet very carefully and removed the lottery ticket. I wanted to have that in my pocket."

"Did you call the paramedics?"

"No, I knew they were busy with Dave and Norma and knew there was no rush."

Detective Morrison removed his cell phone and called the paramedics. He told them to come up to the rental house as soon as they could as there was a problem. He told them it was not an emergency per se, but to come up as quickly as was convenient.

Detective Morrison then excused himself and after getting directions, went up to the bedroom to take a look at Dr. Schroeder. He opened the door and quietly walked over to Jim's body. He verified that there was no pulse, and that Jim was in fact dead. He looked over at Linda, who was sleeping next to him. Detective Morrison decided not to wake her and started to leave the room. Linda sat straight up in the bed and looked at him with a kind of wild look in her eyes.

"Who are you?" she asked, taking quick breaths.

"I'm Detective Morrison," he said. "We've met before."

"What are you doing here in this room?" Linda asked. She then looked over at her husband lying next to her and continued, "Jim, tell him to leave! Jim, Jim." Getting no response she started to shake her dead husband.

Detective Morrison didn't know quite what to do. He wanted to just leave and get out of the room, but he knew he couldn't do that with Linda sitting there shaking her husband.

"Mrs. Schroeder," he said. "Your husband has apparently had a heart attack. We need to get him to the hospital as soon as the paramedics get here."

Linda Schroeder kept shaking her husband and calling his name. The shaking became a little more violent as she started to realize that she was getting no response.

"He's dead," she said. She looked at the detective. "You killed my husband. You killed him."

Jesus, he thought. "No, I didn't kill him. He must have had a heart attack." He felt himself getting very anxious as he looked at her.

"Oh God, oh God," she said and tears started to form at the edges of her eyes.

"Just calm down, Mrs. Schroeder. The paramedics will be here any minute, and maybe they can do something," he said not knowing what else to say. He thought if she continued he was going to have to put her in handcuffs.

She started to shake her dead husband again and started to cry. "Jim, wake up, wake up."

Maybe I can get her to take another sedative. I'll have the paramedics take her to the hospital where they can deal with her until she gets her senses back.

He walked over and looked in the little bag that he thought was the doctor's kit. He searched the bag and found a few black and yellow pills. He thought those must be the pills that Dr. Schroeder was giving his wife as they were the only pills in the bag. He went to the bathroom and got a glass of water. When he came back, she was calming down and looked like she may go back to sleep.

"Here, take this sedative," he said. He walked up to her and in a calming voice told her that everything was going to be all right. He gave her the pill, and she took it with some water. She lay back on the bed almost asleep again. Detective Morrison put the glass back and quickly left the room and went back downstairs.

"What was going on up there? We thought we heard Linda talking to you," George asked.

"Mrs. Schroeder woke up while I was examining her husband," Detective Morrison responded. "She was kind of wild and a little out of her mind. I gave her another sedative, and she went back to sleep. I think she needs to go to the hospital and get some treatment for a few days in order to cope with all that has happened."

"You gave her a sedative?" asked Debbie. "How did you know what to give her?"

"I found some pills in the doctor's small medical bag. They were the only pills in there so they must be what she has been taking. She's going to be quiet for a little while."

As they were standing there, the paramedics knocked on the door and entered the house.

"Where do you want us?" one of them asked.

"I'll show you the room," George said, and started to lead the paramedics up to the Schroeder's room. As they stepped into the room they were shocked to see that Linda had vomited several times and was lying on the bed motionless. The paramedics looked at her and her husband and mumbled, "What the hell?" One paramedic went over to Linda and the other one went to the other side of the bed to look at Jim. After examining Linda, the one paramedic decided she was dead.

"I'm no doctor," one of the paramedics said. "But it looks like she was poisoned with something,"

"This guy has expired also," the other paramedic said.

George was kind of in a daze. He thought for a moment and said, "We think Dr. Schroeder died of a heart attack about a half an hour or so ago." He hesitated and continued, "His wife must have woken up, realized what had happened and took what she thought was another sedative, when it was some kind of poison. She has been a little out of her mind because of all the deaths that have happened here in the last couple of days."

"Maybe," one of the paramedics said. "We need to get the

medical examiner up here to confirm all of this and take a look at the scene. Is the detective still down stairs?"

"Yes," George said. "I'll go down and get him and tell him to come up."

As he left the room, George's mind was racing. When he reached the living room, he looked at the detective and said, "There are two dead bodies upstairs. Linda's dead also. She died of some kind of poison." He looked at the detective. "Do you know for sure what kind of pill that was that you gave her?"

Detective Morrison looked shocked. "I thought it was a sedative. My God, did I give her something else?"

"Apparently you did," George responded.

"Jesus, Christ Almighty. I thought it was the same sedative that the doctor was giving her. It was entirely an accident," he said still looking shocked and shaking a little.

"Look detective, I told the paramedics that she probably was distraught finding her husband dead in bed and got up and took the pill herself."

Detective Morrison looked at George, "Why did you do that?"

"I figured that if we forgot about the pill you gave her, you would forget about all of us buying the lottery ticket."

"It was an accident. I will not be arrested, besides I have you two to witness that I told you about the pill and that at the time I thought it was a sedative."

"Yes, you told us that. And maybe you will not be arrested, but I doubt if the sheriff's department will want to keep you on, knowing that you administered a pill to a female that turned out to be poison."

Detective Morrison stood there and looked at George. Several things were going on in his mind and he didn't say anything.

"Remember all of the reasons we asked you to be quiet before. They still apply. My wife and I are going up to our room and pack as we're leaving as soon as we can. Think it over detective. By not saying anything it's a win, win situation for both of us. By the way, the paramedics have called the medical examiner and are waiting for you up in the bedroom."

George walked over and took Debbie by the hand. They both walked out of the room and went up to pack their things.

Detective Morrison stood there for a moment then walked up to the Schroeder's bedroom. He greeted the paramedics, and told them he understood that they suspected Mrs. Schroeder died of some type of poison. He put on some rubber gloves and walked around the room like he was going to inspect things and picked up the glass he had touched. He made sure neither paramedic was looking and wiped his fingerprints off the glass. He continued to act as if he was investigating the scene and opened the mirrored cabinet above the bathroom sink. He stood there for a moment looking at the small vile of pills.

Damn, he thought. *This is where the doctor put the sedative what he was giving his wife.*

He closed the mirror and walked over to the small medical bag and wiped it where he had touched it. He pulled out the vial out of which he had taken the pill. There were a couple of pills still in the vile. He pulled one out and examined it. He noticed that on the small black and yellow pill had the word "cyanide" stamped in it.

"This must have been the vile she used when she took the pill," he said. "She died of cyanide poisoning."

CHAPTER 39

As George and Debbie Mitchell were putting their bags in their car, Taylor Decker drove up. As Taylor walked up to them, he noticed the ambulance parked outside the rental house.

"I'm Taylor Decker," he said as he held out his hand to George.

"George Mitchell," George responded as he took his hand. "My wife Debbie," as he nodded toward his wife. "As I told you over the phone, we're so sorry that you have lost your parents. They were good people and good friends of ours."

"Why is the ambulance here?" asked Taylor.

"We've had a very unfortunate morning," George responded. "Earlier Dave Wheeler and his wife were killed in a car accident. Our other friends, Jim and Linda Schroeder, also have passed away. It seems that Jim had a heart attack and his wife took some poison by mistake."

Taylor stood there looking at George and Debbie. "Damn, that's four couples who have died out of the five couples who have come up here."

"I took the liberty of packing your parents things. I thought it would save you some time. I didn't think you would want to go through their things this early as it would be too painful," Debbie added.

"Yeah, thanks," Taylor said. "Has the detective determined what really happened yet?" he asked.

"Detective Morrison is upstairs with the paramedics."

"He indicated there may have been foul play in my father's death," Taylor said.

"You can talk to the detective about that. Even if there was, which I understand there is some questions about that, it doesn't matter because the suspected individual died last night," George said.

"I think it does matter," responded Taylor. "We need to determine why Mr. Bellows would want to harm my parents."

"I don't think we'll ever know. It is just a terrible circumstance, all of which no one understands," relayed George. "Maybe there was some kind of problem between them that none of us knew about. Debbie and I don't know of any possible reason. I'm sure Detective Morrison will agree with me, but you need to talk to him yourself."

Taylor looked at both of them and said, "I don't know of any problems either. My parents never talked about any problems. All I ever heard was what a good time they had when they came up here to Russell Cove. I don't have any idea why Fred Bellows would do such a thing."

"We're still not really sure he did anything," George responded.

"Well, anyway thanks for being my parents' friends all these years. I'm going upstairs now to discuss this with the detective. I'll abide by what he says in his report."

George and Debbie watched him go in the house.

"What do you think Detective Morrison will tell him?" Debbie asked her husband.

"I think he'll tell him the same thing we told him," George said. "We'll never know what Fred Bellows had against Tom and Pam Decker. The rest of the deaths were terrible accidents. Let's go."

CHAPTER 40

Taylor Decker moved into the house and stood in the hallway. He heard voices upstairs so he followed the sounds. He came to a bedroom where he saw three people. Two of the individuals were paramedics working on what looked like a man and a woman. The other individual was inspecting the room and was wearing a pair of rubber gloves. The gloved individual looked up and saw Taylor.

"Sorry sir, you cannot enter the room as we're trying to get things organized."

"I'm Taylor Decker. Are you Detective Morrison?"

Detective Morrison stopped what he was doing and looked at Taylor. "That's right."

"Can we go somewhere and talk? I'd like to ask you a few questions," Taylor asked.

Detective Morrison hesitated for a moment, looked at the paramedics and said, "You guys can take it from here. I'll be downstairs if you need me for anything else. The medical examiner will be here any moment."

Detective Morrison and Taylor walked downstairs and sat down in the living room. Neither one of them said anything for a moment.

"Detective can you tell me what happened to my parents?"

Detective Morrison sat there for a moment trying to gather his thoughts. He looked at Taylor and said, "First of all, as I said on the phone, I'm very sorry for what has happened. It must be a terrible and sudden loss for you."

Taylor didn't say anything.

Detective Morrison went on, "Let's start with your father. We suspect that Fred Bellows may have caused your father's death. It looks like Mr. Bellows may have hit your father with a golf club, then broke his neck. He tried to make it look like an accident by wedging a golf club in the golf cart so it would run down a hill and roll off over a steep bank."

Taylor didn't say anything. He sat there staring out the living room window.

"The report I received from your mother's accident indicated that someone drained the brake fluid from her car. I'm sure the accident was caused by brake failure."

Finally, Taylor turned toward Detective Morrison and asked, "Do you think Fred Bellows had anything to do with the accident?"

"He was alone in the house for over an hour after your father's accident. He had plenty of time to drain the fluid from you mother's car and pull the fuses."

"Did you question him about all this? Did you find out why he would do such a thing?"

"I gathered enough evidence to bring him to the station house for questioning. I was going to do that this morning, but last night he and his wife were killed in an accident here at the house. I thought you might shed some light on the reason Mr. Bellows would want to kill your parents."

"I met them a couple of times. I knew they were long-time friends from college. I don't have any idea why Fred Bellows would do such a thing."

"As it stands right now, I guess we'll never know. Maybe Bellows had a long-time grudge against your parents," Detective Morrison said.

"What about the other deaths? Are any of them related to what happened to my parents?"

"I'm ruling the death of Fred and Ginger Bellows an accident. For some reason they didn't take the proper precautions when they set an electric wine chiller next to the Jacuzzi. Somehow it fell into the water."

"I understand Mr. Wheeler and his wife are also dead. Was that an accident too?" asked Taylor Decker.

"It's a little early to tell. It looks like Mr. Wheeler was going for fuel and had some kind of a blackout. He hit his wife and ran off the road, killing them both. There will be an autopsy on him, but even if he had a small stroke, it will be very difficult to detect. I'm not even sure if he wasn't trying to commit suicide and take his wife with him."

"What about Dr. Schroeder and his wife?" Taylor asked.

"The medical examiner has not arrived yet. Everything we see indicates that Dr. Schroeder had a heart attack. We know his wife was extremely distraught over all these accidents. We believe she took a cyanide pill when she thought she was taking a sedative to calm herself down."

"A cyanide pill? Why did the Doctor have cyanide pills?"

"We don't know the answer to that either. Not sure it matters now anyway."

Taylor sat there for a minute, then said, "What about George Mitchell? He is the only one that's OK. Do you suspect him of anything?"

"Mr. Mitchell and his wife were in Sebastopol when your father had his accident. They were never alone in this house prior to your mother's accident. They were at dinner with two of the couples when the Jacuzzi accident occurred. They were next to Mr. Wheeler's wife when she was hit by the car, and they certainly did not cause Dr. Schroeder to have a heart attack. George and Debbie Mitchell had nothing to do with any of these unfortunate happenings."

"Did he have any answers as to why Bellows would want to kill my parents?" asked Taylor.

"He was in the dark as much as anyone else."

"Is there anything I can do?" asked Taylor.

"The best thing for you to do is take care of your family. I'm sure that's what your parents would want you to do in this situation."

Taylor sat there for another moment, looking out the window. "I guess I'll go get their things and start making arrangements to get them home."

CHAPTER 41

<u>**SIX MONTHS LATER**</u>

George and Debbie Mitchell were relaxing in their wide seats in the first class section of American Airlines flight 155 to Europe. This was their first trip to Europe, and they were looking forward to the three weeks of an organized tour.

Although it has been six months since their time at Russell Cove, Debbie didn't take long walks anymore. She couldn't walk around her neighborhood without bad memories flooding back into her mind. Sometimes she and George walked in shopping malls where there were other things to look at. Other times they would put their iPods in their ears and work out in the two stationary bicycles they had purchased.

A few weeks after they had returned home from Russell Cove they had contacted the children of their friends who died. Each couple had children except Dr. and Linda Schroeder. They explained that they had inherited some money, and that they felt bad about what happened to their parents. Each of the couples had been their good friends. To help with their loss, George and Debbie gave each individual family member twelve thousand dollars. They informed the family members they would give each member this amount each year, or whatever was the maximum amount that was allowable without being taxed. The family members were very appreciative of their efforts. All of them were pleased that they would receive this money as gifts.

George and Debbie also set up educational scholarships for the grandchildren of three of the four families. The scholarships were going to be enough to get them through any college of their choice at the time they were old enough to go.

They read somewhere that Wilt Morrison had quit his job with the sheriff's department. He had taken employment as a security guard at a large winery. They sent Wilt and his wife each a check for twelve thousand dollars and thanked him for all the fine work he did while they were going through their difficult time at Russell Cove. George and Debbie were not really surprised when the checks were returned with a note that said, "Thanks, but no thanks."

When they had cashed in their lottery ticket, they wanted to remain anonymous, which the lottery commission respected. Of course the IRS had to know about their winnings and any other taxing agency, but the newspapers did not publish their names. Both George and Debbie had heard that the good citizens of Russell Cove were still trying to find out which of their friends and neighbors had won the money. They were looking for some kind of change in life style or other hint of wealth but so far had not noticed anything.

As George moved the back of his airline seat further back, he sipped on his drink and thought about the whole situation. He thought maybe someday he would write a book about those three days he spent with his friends and how the murders occurred. He put the thought out of his mind as he was convinced that no one would believe it.

ABOUT THE AUTHOR

Howard Blair was born and raised in the high sierra country in Northern California. After graduating from the University of California, Davis with a degree in Psychology, he married Patricia, his current wife of 46 years. Howard spent three years as an Infantry Officer in the United States Marine Corps, serving some time in Viet Nam in 1964. In 1966 he joined Caterpillar Tractor Co. and was sent to Europe for five and a half years. When he left Caterpillar in 1977, he was an Assistant Divisional Sales Manager of their lift truck subsidiary. He has been the Vice President and General Manager for three Caterpillar Dealers in California, retiring in 2005 from the Caterpillar Dealer covering San Diego and Hawaii. He has served on the Board of Directors of construction associations and college foundations. He currently is the Marketing Manager for the Camp Pendleton Historical Society and the President of the local chapter of the American Cut Glass Association. Because of his extensive management experience, his first book, *Don't be a Dead Fish,* covered topics such as leadership, business planning, suggestions for success, and handling effective meetings. Howard and his wife Patricia live in the San Diego Area.

Printed in the United States
123632LV00002B/1-6/P